Revenge for a Hanging

Bush Creek's hardened Marshal Mason finds his life under threat in his own jail, but he is saved by a young fugitive he had arrested on charges of abduction, horse theft and murder.

When the youngster confesses that he knifed an uncle who had brutally lynched his father, the marshal realizes that he also has a personal interest in settling the long-standing feud that was behind the hanging. Together, the marshal and his young rescuer seek retribution – but final justice can only come after further violence and more deaths.

Revenge for a Hanging

Richard Smith

A Black Horse Western

ROBERT HALE · LONDON

ISBN 978-0-7090-9193-6

Robert Hale Limited
Clerkenwell House
Clerkenwell Green
London EC1R 0HT

www.halebooks.com

Typeset by
Derek Doyle & Associates, Shaw Heath
Printed and bound in Great Britain by
CPI Antony Rowe, Chippenham and Eastbourne

CHAPTER ONE

As the boot crunched into his father's body, Rory Rimmer involuntarily winced and averted his eyes from the brutal beating he was being forced to watch.

Another vicious kick went in but Rory's desperate desire to intervene continued to be frustrated by the pitchfork prongs pressed against his stomach. 'For pity's sake, stop your brothers before they kill him,' he pleaded with the grim-faced man who was effectively keeping him away from the drama taking place on the dusty ground just a few feet away.

To Rory's relief, his plea was acknowledged by his captor. 'Dave and Jake – that's enough. You can see he's well and truly beat. Let him be.'

At that point Jake stood back, but the elder of the two assailants couldn't resist once more thudding his foot into the nearly still body crushed on the ground, before he accepted his brother's advice from the sidelines. Then he deliberately kicked dry earth into Jack Rimmer' s face before turning towards young Rory.

5

'Better help your pa,' he said, signalling that the pitchfork restraint could now be withdrawn. 'Bastard had it coming.' He grunted, spat on the ground, turned and then walked away from the inert body without a backward glance.

At first Jack Rimmer had been getting the better of the full-blooded fistfight with his brother-in-law, David Pritchard. But then David's two brothers and Jack's son Rory had heard the commotion and rushed to the scene. Immediately, Jake Pritchard had gone to join in the fight, whilst Frank had grabbed a pitchfork leaning against a barn and used it to prevent Rory going to his father's aid.

For a while Jack had still been able to hold his own in the uneven two-against-one battle. He had already struck some hefty blows against David, but when Jake had joined in he found himself receiving more punishment than he could himself deliver. Eventually he weakened under the attack from both directions and slipped to the ground under a barrage of blows.

The fight had been brewing for over two decades. Even as a child, Rory had been aware that his father had never got along with his wife's eldest brother, David Pritchard. He had frequently heard them arguing, but he now found it a struggle to accept that the long-standing differences between the two men could have led to the scene he was forced to witness. Whilst it was true that there were years of mutual dislike and verbal assault behind the fistfight, it still seemed incomprehensible to the youngster that his uncle's enmity should have escalated to this level of violence.

After Rory had managed to get his father inside and clean him up, he suggested that they should call in the doctor to carry out a thorough examination, but Jack had resisted.

'I'll be OK, son,' he had insisted. 'Don't reckon there's anything broke. Coupla days I'll be as good as new, you'll see. Then we're gettin' outa here. Your uncle David is wrong about most things, but he's right about that. There's no reason for us to stay now your dear mother has gone. She was the only reason I stayed in the first place, all those years ago. Her brothers have always resented me being here and I'm afraid that has rubbed off on their feelings for you, too.'

Three days later they rode out from Peterland Valley without a word to anyone except the old gravedigger, who was at the local cemetery when they went to pay their last respects to Rory's mother, Ann.

'You boys quittin'?' asked the old man, who always seemed to know everyone's business, as well as every family's history over the last sixty years or so. He got no direct answer to his blunt question, but drew his own conclusion from their dress and the extra horse, which was obviously carrying provisions.

Later that day he didn't hesitate to confirm David Pritchard's guess that the father and son had indeed made the grave their last stop before heading off along the trail out of town in a southerly direction.

Resting from his exertions, the old man recalled

that there had been a family row about the inscription on the grave's headstone. The original request from Jack Rimmer to the stonemason had simply been: 'Ann Rimmer. Deeply missed by a loving husband and son'. But the Pritchards had insisted that her marriage didn't erase the importance of her original surname and had demanded that the stonemason added 'and the whole Pritchard family'.

Remembering that the dispute had meant that the hastily revised marker had been produced only half an hour before the burial, the gravedigger – who carried no brief for any of the parties involved – was quite happy to take David Pritchard's money in exchange for information about the Rimmers' departure.

'Sure didn't look to me as if they had any intention of coming back,' he volunteered, when Pritchard asked whether they were equipped for a long journey. 'Sure bet they wasn't just out for a little mornin' exercise. The way they stood over that grave looked to me like a final farewell.'

'That's what I figured,' said Pritchard. He departed with a grim look on his face.

CHAPTER TWO

Except for an occasional shake of its head, the horse stayed still. Perhaps, after the hard morning's ride, it was simply enjoying the ample shade from the leafy branches above it.

Or maybe it sensed that a man's life depended on its actions.

It would certainly have been aware of the weight on its back, but perhaps it was puzzled by the complete lack of movement from its owner, Jack Rimmer, as he sat astride it with his hands tied behind him. Six minutes passed. Seven minutes. Then, inevitably, the animal shifted slightly. It was only a couple of steps forward and to the side, but it was sufficient movement to cause the man to slip from the saddle and leave his whole body weight suspended on the end of the rope looped around his neck. Instinctively he writhed and twisted in a vain effort to find some kind of foothold, but that only had the effect of tightening the noose and causing a rasping moan to escape from his throat, despite the necktie bound round his mouth.

This was not to be a quick, efficient hanging. Not for this man the jerking neck-break usually associated with the sudden fall of a gallows trapdoor. For him there was not even the easing of pain which could sometimes come from family or other sympathizers being allowed to pull on the suspended legs in order to tighten the noose more speedily.

This, instead, was going to be the slowest form of strangulation, with the rope only gradually tightening and cutting off the supply of air as the windpipe became steadily compressed. A hanging was never pleasant, but this one was to be particularly drawn out.

As the man's suffering continued, he had three observers.

Two were the men who, a few minutes earlier, had strung the rope over one of a tree's stronger branches, fixed the noose around their victim's neck and struggled to manoeuvre him on to the saddle of his own horse. He had still been slightly dazed from the rifle-butt blow he had received to the back of his head, so they had simply held the horse and waited until their victim fully regained his senses. They watched silently as he shook his head and immediately felt the coarse rope biting into the flesh of his neck. He froze as he understood his predicament, fully expecting his tormentors to end his life by sending the horse on its way with a slap or a gunshot. Instead, they had walked away to leave their victim sitting on the animal with his hands bound, waiting for the big chestnut's inevitable movement.

Now they simply looked on as Jack Rimmer's life gradually ebbed away. They seemed neither elated nor regretful at the effects of their actions. They sat, without speaking, on a fallen log, watching the man's small movements become less frequent and less pronounced.

The third observer was far more emotionally involved. This was not surprising, for it was Rory Rimmer's own father who was dying so slowly and painfully in front of him.

Left lying on the ground with his hands and feet roughly tied, the nineteen-year-old could do nothing to influence the scene being played out not ten yards away. He couldn't even cry out or speak, because – like his father – he had his mouth gagged, so that the two could not communicate with each other or protest to their assailants. He could only look on in frustrated horror, as he struggled to keep back the sobs he guessed would simply have given sadistic amusement to the two executioners now watching his father's life evaporate. Despite the limitations to his physical movement, however, Rory was aware that, within him, there was significant emotional change. Bewilderment and pain were transforming into cold, hard anger.

As his father's breathing eased and then ceased altogether when the trachea finally closed, Rory's incredulity hardened into an overwhelming bitterness. It was only a few days since his mother's sudden

11

death. Now his father's life had been taken, too, and Rory's hatred towards the uncle responsible for this second loss reached a depth of loathing he would never have imagined himself capable of feeling.

'What we gonna do with the kid, boss?' asked the taller and less well-dressed of the two men as he stood up and stretched himself. 'Do you want me to leave him tied up here or get him on his horse?'

'I'll deal with him in a minute, Ned,' replied the older man, still sitting on the log. 'You just check that bastard over there has finally choked it. He took long enough, didn't he?'

'Yep. But I reckon he's had it now, boss.' As he spoke, the gangly Ned Pointing limped over and prodded somewhat gingerly at the suspended body. It swung gently sideways as a result of his action, without any movement of its own volition. The body, which – only fifteen minutes earlier – had been a man, was now a corpse. 'He won't be doin' no more runnin' away,' Ned added.

'Serves him right,' replied his still-seated employer. Slowly, he rose and walked over to Rory Rimmer. Then, without warning, he viciously kicked his nephew in his side as he lay on the ground. 'Now it's your turn,' he snarled.

Ned looked aghast at his companion's comment. 'You ain't gonna kill him, too?' he asked in alarm.

'What choice we got? He's seen us hang his father and we can't leave him to tell his tale.'

'But he ain't done nothing,' Ned protested.

'Don't matter. He's not gonna stay alive to talk to the law. But we'll make it a quicker end for him. I'll even let him face me like a man when I put a bullet in him.'

Ned opened his mouth, ready to offer further complaint, but the look on his employer's face persuaded him that further objections were pointless.

Rory groaned from the kick he had received, but watched carefully as his assailant used a long-bladed Mexican knife to cut the rope that bound his feet and then casually stabbed the knife into the trunk of the tree that still supported his father's suspended body.

Pritchard pulled the youngster roughly to his feet and punched him viciously in the stomach before spinning him round to get at the other rope knotted behind his back. Rory staggered to one side, so that Pritchard had to steady him with his left hand whilst releasing the rope with his right. As the binding fell free Rory deliberately staggered one more step sideways, reached for the knife and quickly jabbed it into the other man's belly. He was surprised how easily the blade penetrated the flesh.

Blood seeped from the wound as Rory pulled the knife free but clearly it had not penetrated any vital organs, for his uncle was still able to grab at Rory's throat with surprising strength. Twisting away from Pritchard, Rory stabbed again, ignoring the expression of shocked horror in his uncle's eyes as he grabbed at Rory for support. Even as Pritchard released his grip and his body slumped down towards the ground, Rory stabbed for a third time. This time the blade simply caught his uncle's shoulder as he fell, but it was a blow that was not needed. David Pritchard's blood was slowly spreading a crimson stain on the ground around his still body.

Rory's attention turned towards Ned, the other unofficial hangman. The ranch hand had been moving away towards the four tethered horses while his boss had been untying the youngster. Now, aware that there was some unplanned action going on behind him, he turned and quickly sized up the situation. At the same instant as Ned started to draw his Colt from its holster, Rory threw the knife.

His aim was well off target but the action was enough to cause Ned to duck instinctively. As he did so, his foot caught on a tree root and his pistol fired aimlessly into the air as he fell to the ground.

Rory panicked. Without a weapon and undefended, he grabbed his father's horse and mounted whilst Ned gathered his wits, pulled himself to his feet, and looked round for his dropped revolver.

Another shot rang out as Rory urged the chestnut out of Ned's range and away from the scene where his father had just died so violently. He rode blindly, not knowing or caring where he was headed but simply seeking to put space between himself and Ned's bullets.

For around twenty minutes he rode across the flat terrain with hardly a glance behind him, until he reached a slight rise in the ground. Once there he acknowledged that his father's horse, though a strong and gutsy animal, was struggling. Its neck and shoulders were wet with salty sweat and its breath was rasping. He had been ridden hard, perhaps too hard. It was time to ease off, so Rory brought the animal to a halt and took the opportunity to scan the seemingly endless scrubland territory behind him. Just the occasional clump of trees were scattered across this mixed brush country, and they did not prevent him achieving a good view and satisfying himself that there were no signs of pursuit.

Then, as he thought through the situation a little more clearly, he came to the conclusion that it was unlikely that Ned would have started the chase by himself. He was, after all, only a hired hand. No, Rory told himself, Ned's action would almost certainly have been to report back to his other bosses: the two brothers of the man Rory Rimmer had knifed. And there was no doubting their response. They would hunt down the nephew who had killed their sibling. They, like their brother David, had harboured no love for Rory's father, and now they would have good cause to extend their hostility to his son.

CHAPTER THREE

As Rory walked his father's weary horse the sticky heat of the day diminished. He, too, was tired and hungry, but powerless to do much about it. The two attackers had taken his own revolver and removed his father's rifle from the horse's scabbard, so he had nothing with which to secure himself a freshmeat meal. Even worse, he had little water and he doubted that he would easily find any in the mixture of mesquite, dwarf oak and other wild scrub. He remounted and rode slowly for a further hour or so, with the chestnut's pace becoming increasingly laboured. Rory knew that any properly fed and watered pursuers would have no trouble gaining on him, but he felt confident that by the time Ned returned to the ranch and told his story he would have a substantial lead on anyone tracking him.

With his father he had travelled for two and a half days before David Pritchard had caught up with them, so – thinking more rationally now – he realized he probably had at least a four-day start. As the sun started to set he approached gently rising ground and decided that he would rest up by a small outcrop of rocks. Although most of the provisions had been left behind with the spare horse, his saddle-bag contained a meagre amount of dried food. It was enough to keep him going.

Throughout a seemingly endless night he was beset by vivid recollections of the day's horrors. He slept only in short spells and found himself awakening with sweat on his brow, despite the chill of the night air. He set off very early the next morning, with his own parched mouth and empty stomach worrying him less than his concern for the horse's welfare. Both he and the animal were in poor condition but there was no alternative to pushing on slowly across the mostly flat scrubland.

He had no clear idea of how far he had travelled, but knew that his early panicky rush to get away from Ned Pointing had meant that he had pushed the chestnut too hard at the beginning of his flight. He had to compensate now by allowing his mount to make only steady progress. With no particular destination in mind, Rory simply made sure that he was consistently moving in a westward direction, away from possible pursuit. Gradually, though, the ground rose and he could see a line of hills a few miles off. He altered his direction slightly and headed towards this higher land, the Frimley Ridge, where he was relieved to find a shallow stream running down from the higher level. He allowed the horse to slake its immediate thirst and did the same himself, then he rested awhile before taking more water and washing away the blood that had baked hard on the hand he had used to stab his uncle.

He found an easy route through the range of rounded hills, but at one point he climbed higher to gain a clear view of the land he had covered that morning. Standing high in his stirrups, he satisfied himself that, at least for now, there was no one in sight. He now felt really confident that there had been no immediate pursuit and that his calculation that Ned would have returned to the ranch was justified. He descended carefully to the lower plain on the other side of the hills, stopping briefly to sustain himself with a little dried meat from his saddle-bag. The jerky, which he softened in his mouth for ages before swallowing it, would be all he would get that day.

By mid-afternoon on the second day, with the sun burning down on the rider and his tired mount, they hit upon a stage trace running diagonally across the westerly route Rory had been taking. Gratefully, he turned on to the rough trail, knowing that the wagon tracks must ultimately lead him to some sort of township.

He knew his immediate ordeal was over, but the grim prospect of future reprisal for his own actions left Rory Rimmer more than fearful as his sore eyes made out a group of buildings in the distance.

CHAPTER FOUR

GOOD CLEAN ROOMS proclaimed the sign outside
the small hotel, but young Rory Rimmer was instinctively wise enough to know not to hand over money
unless he had checked the accommodation on offer
with his own eyes. Common sense indicated that,
even if it achieved nothing else, forcefully demanding a personal inspection ensured that you were
likely to be offered the best of the few rooms avail-
able.

In the event, he was satisfied. The room he was
shown was not large, and was minimally furnished. In
addition to the bed, there was a wardrobe and a
dresser, and a table with a basin and pitcher of water.
The walls were plain, with a few hooks nailed into
them. However, the room was at the end of a corri-
dor and, which was important, had a single sash
window overlooking Bush Creek's main street. This
was probably not an advantage in terms of being able
to sleep through any outside noise, but it gave him a
chance to observe what was happening below.

'OK?' asked the bored and tired-looking mestizo who had somewhat unwillingly trudged up the single flight of stairs to the room with a chalked number '4' scrawled on the door.

'OK,' replied Rory. It was hardly a stimulating exchange, but was sufficient to serve both men's lack of desire for further communication.

As he laid out the few belongings he had with him Rory paid little attention to the mixed smell of tobacco and stale sweat which pervaded the room. The pungent odour was inevitable when many previous occupants had slumbered there after long days and nights in the saddle. It usually took several hot bath sessions to remove the natural smells from riders' bodies, and many did not have the time, money or inclination to enjoy such luxuries.

Physically exhausted, Rory slumped on to the bed, intending to have a short rest as the evening darkness set in. Despite his aching limbs, however, his mind remained active as he pondered his position and tried to decide what to do.

His natural law-abiding inclination was to seek out the town marshal and unburden himself by recounting in full the dreadful story of his father's death and his own desperate retribution. But even in his disturbed mental state he recognized that there was an obvious danger in this straightforward approach. How could he be confident that his version of events would be believed? The lawman would need proof, and proof was something Rory was in no position to provide.

He was not even confident that he could find his way back to the scene of the hanging. Even if he could succeed in retracing the route of his panic-stricken escape, there could be no certainty that there would be any physical evidence to support his story. He thought it was entirely possible – indeed even probable – that the bodies of his father and uncle would be removed from the immediate scene of death. Any marshal or county sheriff investigating the crime would eventually find himself facing a straight contest between Rory's word and that of the only other witness, the ranch hand Ned, who would doubtless come up with a story which incriminated Rory but exonerated himself and David Pritchard.

Pressed by his employers and eager to avoid attaching any blame to himself, Ned could invent any version of events he chose. He could, Rory acknowledged, completely deny that the hanging had taken place and even argue that Rory and his father had together killed David Pritchard and then simply ridden off in different directions to hinder pursuit.

Rory figured that by talking to the marshal he might simply incriminate himself without ever being able to prove that the knifing had been a defensive action following the hanging. Faced with Rory's voluntary confession, any lawman would have no choice but to hold him ready for trial with perhaps little, if any, chance that the full truth would ever come out.

As his frenzied brain continued its troubled reasoning, Rory accepted that there was one other factor of paramount importance: the simple fact that he could never return to the home he and his father had so recently left. His remaining two uncles would never allow that.

Rory made his decision. Though it was clearly the right course of action, going to the marshal seemed to pose more threat to Rory himself than it did to anyone else. However things might turn out, he could never return to his old life. The best practical course of action, he reluctantly decided, was to put the past behind him and ride off to a new life – even if it effectively turned him into a fugitive.

So, although Rory needed a rest and intended to get himself at least one good soak in a barbershop tub, he now decided that he had no intention of hanging around in Bush Creek longer than neces-sary. With his mind made up, he was anxious to put as many miles as possible behind him. Remaining too long in one place was not part of his newly formed plan.

Besides, he knew that the longer he stayed in town the more likely it was that people would be able to remember his face or his clothes. Then they could subsequently recall him if questioned by any venge-ful riders, or lawmen, who might be following.

In any case, it didn't take Rory long to decide that, even if he had not been on the run from possible pursuit, Bush Creek was not somewhere he would particularly have wanted to stay. It had the feel of a town in decay, with the false-fronted buildings looking in dire need of care and attention, and the whole place seeming to operate at an unexciting leisurely pace.

As he had sought out the town's only livery stable, he had quickly sized up Bush Creek's lack of prosperity. It was perhaps best summed up by a peeled-paint sign reading BANK but with a chalked note alongside adding: 'Closed for good'.

Walking his tired chestnut the length of the main street, he noted the usual premises of a small town – an eating-house, two strangely silent saloons, a couple of general stores, both seemingly closed in the early evening, and an undertaker. Except for the three horses hitched out front of one of the saloons, there was no sign of any coming and going from outside the town. There were few people about and Rory was pleased to note that those who were out on the rutted main street hardly bothered to pay him any attention. He hoped that he could remain fairly anonymous before pushing away from any pursuers, though he had no idea where he would be heading. Other than once expressing a vague desire to see the Rio Grande, his father had not indicated any particular destination and – in his flight – Rory had been concerned simply with getting away from the scene of his father's hanging.

He had a vague notion of continuing west through the changing Texas scenery and then turning south towards the river that formed the Mexican border, but for now his forward destination seemed less important than simply putting distance behind him.

CHAPTER FIVE

After his short physical, if not mental, evening's rest, Rory ventured out of the quaintly named Moontime Hotel to get a further feel of the place, pour a couple of much-needed drinks down his parched throat and have a meal.

He chose the least garish-looking of the two saloons on offer and made sure he placed himself in a darkish corner facing the batwing entrance of the large open room, which was used for eating, drinking, gambling, exchanging news and, sometimes, trading insults or even blows – though it was only on very rare occasions these days that physical contact took the place of oral communication.

The saloon was hardly humming. Two drummers sat together at one table, probably discussing the lack of sales opportunities in this unpromising town. At another, four town elders were playing cards, though it looked as if they were simply passing time rather than indulging in any serious gambling. The

24

other, somewhat noisier, occupants were clearly
ranch hands or nesters from outlying homesteads.
The piano stool was unoccupied and there was no
sign of any females, not even a brightly dressed
saloon girl such as one might have expected to be
present.

Rory had been sitting down for around ten
minutes when he became aware of a sudden change
in the atmosphere within the saloon. The already low
conversation noise level dropped a few more deci-
bels as heads turned towards the entrance.

The cause was the arrival of a huge hulk of a man.
He was tall, but appeared almost as wide, with the
broadest of shoulders pushing out from a great
barrel of a chest. His size would have marked him out
in any setting, but his physical bulk was accentuated
by a singularly unattractive facial appearance that
made him instantly a man who, once seen, would
never be forgotten. He had a high forehead, deep
sunken eyes, and a hooked nose – all combining to
present a generally fearsome presence.

His clothes were nondescript except for one significant feature: a marshal's badge pinned to his vest.
All in all, it was hardly surprising that his slow, delib-
erate entrance had a dampening effect on a room
that was supposed to be dedicated to relaxation and
pleasure. Here, clearly, was a man whose presence
would command attention in any setting.

Without haste, Bush Creek's marshal walked to the
bar, where the barkeeper wordlessly placed a tumbler
of whiskey in front of him. This was immediately con-

sumed and the tumbler quickly refilled.

Then the marshal turned and unhurriedly cast his eyes over the room's occupants. A few of those nearest the bar acknowledged his gaze with a nod, a slight wave or even a couple of words, but there was no warmth in any of the greetings. Rory's immediate impression was that the marshal was a man apart, respected for his bulk and his badge of office rather than his character.

As Rory supped at his beer, his gaze remained fixed on the marshal until he became aware, with some trepidation, that his stare was now being reciprocated. The marshal looked him in the eye for what seemed an eternity. Then, his glass still in his left hand, he moved towards Rory. As he did so, a couple of drinkers gently slid their chairs aside to open a clearer passage for the big man to move through until he stood at the other side of Rory's table. He continued to stare down at him in a manner that the youngster found unnerving yet compulsive.

When eventually the marshal spoke the shock of his voice was as great as the previous shock of his appearance. From a man of his bulk the natural expectation was of a gruff, bearlike boom of a voice. Instead, the sound that emanated from him was a squeaky whine. 'What you here in Bush Creek for?' The contrast between the physical appearance and the shrill, unimpressive sound was so great that Rory found himself smiling in disbelief, and certainly not concentrating on the actual words the marshal had spoken. This was an error because, despite the shrill sound, there was no mistaking the irritation and menace in the lawman's second utterance.

'I asked what you was doin' here and I expect an answer.'

Rory, suddenly flustered, didn't know how to reply. What was he doing here? He had already decided against admitting that he was riding away from an incident in which he had knifed a man. He opened his mouth but no words formed as his brain struggled to find an appropriate response.

'Lost your tongue, have you?' taunted the marshal. 'And you're sittin' in my chair and I don't take kindly to that.'

'I, er, didn't know,' Rory stammered. He started to rise in order to give up his seat.

Instantly the marshal's right hand shot to his side and Rory found himself looking down the barrel of what appeared to be a well-used Colt .45.

'You get up real slow,' the marshal whined, 'with your hands on the table and well away from your weapon.'

Rory did exactly what he had been told, adding quickly: 'Look, I ain't carryin' a weapon, Marshal, and I'm real sorry about using your chair. I'm a stranger in town and I just didn't know.'

'Of course you're a stranger. Think I didn't know that? I know everyone within a hundred miles of here and you sure ain't one of them. Now, what are you doin' here?'

'I'm just ridin' through . . . on my way west,' Rory

assured him. 'I ain't plannin' on stayin'.'

'Why not? Don't you like Bush Creek?'

The challenging question was so surprising that Rory was again at a loss to know how he was expected to react. Was he supposed to compliment the marshal on his unremarkable town, or what?

Whilst he hesitated, he was aware that all eyes in the room were upon him. His intended unobtrusiveness had been blown sky high by this very public scrutiny. Everyone in the room would remember this confrontational incident and take note of the slim youth with the mop of curly hair.

'I just didn't intend stoppin' here long, that's all,' he eventually responded lamely.

Replacing his revolver in its holster, the marshal looked Rory up and down carefully. He judged that, despite his slight build, the youngster probably had a wiry strength that matched the firm set of his lightly stubbled jaw. He was dressed plainly in a rancher's clothes and would probably have been thought of by the opposite sex as good-looking.

'Well, young stranger, you just make sure you move on quietly. This is a law-abiding town and I plan to keep it that way. Now you move over there somewhere and let me get at my seat so I can rest my bones.'

'Yessir,' said Rory. 'I was just goin' anyway.' He edged round the table so that the marshal was allowed easy access to his chosen chair, and – carefully stepping round other tables and outstretched legs – headed out of the saloon. He was aware that he had achieved neither of his objectives. He certainly hadn't remained unnoticed and neither had he eaten.

CHAPTER SIX

When he left the saloon, Marshal Mason carried out his usual evening tour of the town to check that all was well. There were very few people about and, satisfied, he returned to his combined office, jail and sleeping quarters.

Unusually, he decided that he would have another drink and pulled a bottle of whiskey from a desk drawer. He also took a small pile of 'Wanted' posters from another drawer and thumbed through them. It was not a very elaborate search, but he just wanted to check that the youngster he had challenged in the saloon was not on the run from another law officer's territory, since there was something about him that seemed familiar. However, his search produced nothing so he put the matter out of his mind and, lulled by the drink, let his thoughts wander back over his earlier life.

Even as a child he had been conscious that his general appearance and distinctive squeaky voice marked him out as someone apart from the crowd, and he had developed a withdrawn and inward-looking personality.

His parents, although fanatically religious-minded, were not a demonstratively loving couple. They concentrated more on their son's basic physical development and religious education, rather than his psychological needs. The doctor had told them that his shrill vocal cords would revert to normal when he reached puberty, but in truth there was no firm basis for this diagnosis and it proved to be utterly misplaced. At first his voice brought forth ridicule from his contemporaries, but he had quickly found that firm use of his bunched fists provided a ready silencer. No one laughed at him a second time.

He found it particularly difficult to relate to the opposite sex. His ugly facial features and swarthy frame did not present an attractive proposition to the local girls and in later life his few experiences of sexual intercourse were all the joyless results of commercial transactions.

Even amongst his male acquaintances he failed to establish any close relationships during his formative period. So it had been somewhat to his surprise that, in his late teenage years, he became associated with a young contemporary he met up with accidentally whilst out riding alone. The two had been approaching a river from different directions and had finished up facing each other from opposite banks.

'Goin' for a swim?' the stranger had shouted across the water as he tied his horse and then

31

stripped off his clothes.

'No, don't think so,' Abraham Mason had replied. He dismounted and sat on the bank, watching as the young man enjoyed the refreshing cool of the water before returning to the other side to dress. Then, rather than riding off, the stranger brought his horse over the river and sat himself down to begin a very one-sided conversation in which Abraham found himself listening to a continuous stream of ideas, statements and beliefs delivered with an amazing enthusiasm and gusto.

He listened in awe and hardly spoke a word except to answer questions put to him by this confident and self-possessed youngster, who seemed to know so much about the world and had already formed strong opinions about a host of subjects Abraham Mason had never even considered. They sat for well over an hour before the stranger said he was going to have another swim, and again suggested that Abraham join him.

Somewhat shamefaced, Abraham admitted that he couldn't swim. No one had ever shown him and he had never thought to try by himself.

'It's easy,' he was assured. 'Come back tomorrow and I'll teach you.'

And so had begun Abraham Mason's first, and only, real friendship.

For nearly a year the two met fairly frequently, spending time in competitive practice with their revolvers, riding and even swimming as Abraham Mason discovered that his broad shoulders and general strength gave him superiority over his erstwhile tutor.

They also spent considerable time simply talking, though their discourse still tended to be rather one-sided, with one particular enthusiasm repeatedly cropping up. Mason's companion was determined 'to see the world', and he became equally determined that the two of them should see it together.

With no particular ties to hold him, Abraham found himself agreeing and, just after his twentieth birthday, he said farewell to his parents and set off on a journey which was to take him over many miles, through the final horrors of a Civil War, into many personal battles, and – another twenty years later – into the town of Bush Creek to take up the role of marshal.

Throughout it all, he remained a self-contained figure. Even his comrades in battle treated him with respect for his physical strength and undoubted courage, rather than sharing anything approaching the strong personal bonding common amongst those facing a shared enemy and the ever-present threats to life.

Unlike others who returned home to loved ones and familiar territory when the Civil War ended in 1865, he never went back. He had mentally rejected his parents' strict Jewish observances as nothing more than a set of rules to be followed as part of the daily grind, and decided that he did not want the rest of his life to be controlled, or even unduly influenced, by their beliefs and customs. Their way of life was consciously discarded when he left home and he had no desire to return to it.

Now, as he poured a further whiskey, he mulled over his past as a soldier, an Indian fighter, a bounty hunter and a legitimized lawman. It was a life that had always encompassed a degree of danger and violence. He had seen many lives ended with an arrow, a lance or a bullet, and it had been his own trigger finger that had often been the cause of injury or death.

This had never troubled him unduly, as he had always considered his actions justified by some kind of moral imperative. He had never acted because of personal malice and had never found himself on the wrong side of the law. His conscience remained clear and he therefore never burdened himself with negative thoughts of regret or self-incrimination. Neither was grief an emotion that visited him with any frequency, though he occasionally found himself wondering what might have happened to his parents or others whose lives had touched his own, even if the relationship had not been a particularly close or intimate one.

Now, as he sipped his whiskey in the Bush Creek marshal's office, he felt settled. It was a relatively easy way of life that – at least for the time being – suited him well, though something in his guts told him that changes might be on the way.

CHAPTER SEVEN

'My horse OK?' queried Rory, as he approached the chestnut.

'Yes, mister. Don't you worry none. I'll pay him good attention.'

In the semi-dark of the livery stable Rory struggled to see the features of his precious animal's carer. He at first assumed that the slim figure and gentle voice belonged to a young lad, but as he moved round to pat the horse's flank, he could see that it was a girl of perhaps sixteen or seventeen years.

'How long you gonna be here?' she asked.

'Not more than a couple of nights.'

'Which way you goin'?'

Rory was immediately cagey. After his experience in the saloon a short while earlier he was now even keener not to volunteer information about himself, and was instantly on his guard when faced with these direct questions about his movements.

'Kinda nosy, aren't you?' he asked, without too much roughness in his voice.

'Sorry, mister. Didn't mean to poke into your business. It's just that I'm so damned tired with Bush Creek that I like to hear about other places. Whichever way you're plannin' on travellin', it must be better than stayin' here.'

'I wouldn't bet on it,' replied Rory, softening his attitude a little, despite himself. Surely this young girl was harmless enough. 'There are far worse places to be than here,' he added.

'You been to worse places then?' she asked. 'At least you must have seen things.'

'What *things*?' There was a mixed hint of amusement and caution in Rory's voice.

'Oh! I don't know. Just things. How would I know? I don't really remember anywhere 'cept this dump of a town and the few miles of scrubby sagebrush and mesquite around the river bend. Nothing to see, and not much to do 'cept ride around a bit.' She paused, then: 'Can I ride your horse out a bit tomorrow, mister?'

'No you can't.' Suspicion, roughness and irritation were now all encompassed in Rory's reply. 'He needs a rest even more than I do. Leave him be, and I'll be in tomorrow to make sure you're treating him well. Mind you do!'

He gave a last couple of pats to his animal's side, then turned and left without a further comment or farewell. Though still hungry, he decided that it was time to return to the Moontime Hotel.

The next morning, after another fitful sleep, in

which he was still debating with himself about the immediate past and his uncharacteristic decision not to tell his story to the marshal, Rory arrived early at the stable and was surprised to find the girl again seated on a rough wooden stool.

'You been here all night?' he asked, as his nostrils became accustomed to the mixed smells of hay and fresh manure.

'No, but I like to get here early to make sure the horses are OK. You taking yours out today, mister?'

'No, I told you he's had a hard ride, and deserves a rest. Might just walk him round a bit.'

'I'll do it, mister. No need for you to bother. I'll do it.'

Rory hesitated. He quite liked the idea of not having to make himself too visible with his mount. His encounter with the marshal the previous evening had already made him more recognizable than he would have liked, and it was preferable not to be seen around too much. Casual observers were more likely to remember a man and his horse together, and be able to provide a description to any questioners.

'Why you so keen to take my horse out?' he asked.

She smiled, thought for a minute, and then gave what he judged to be an honest answer. 'Well,' she said, 'I just like being with horses and feeling how they respond – and there's another thing, too. You might just decide to pay me a bit extra when you leave.'

Rory returned her smile. There was an open quality about the girl that was hard not to respond to.

Despite his careful reticence, he found himself relaxing somewhat and reacting favourably to her naturally friendly manner.

'Could be,' he replied. 'So long as you don't expect too much.'

'Don't worry, mister. I'll look after your horse real good. You sure you don't want me to ride him out – just a bit?'

'No,' he replied. 'A gentle walk will do.'

Clearly disappointed, she stood up and went to the big chestnut and confidently caressed him. The animal immediately responded by nuzzling up to her, clearly appreciating the kind of attention he was getting.

'I'll take him out soon,' she said, 'before there's too many folk about. Then I'll give him a good brush down. Think he'd like that.'

'OK,' replied Rory. 'I'll go get something to eat, then come back later.'

Keeping a low profile, whilst making sure he didn't actually look furtive, Rory did as he had indicated – accepting how hungry he was after missing his meal the previous night. Obviously his body was desperate to put back some of the energy reserves he had used up on his journey to Bush Creek. In the town's only eating-house, other than the two saloons, he ate a hearty breakfast and was pleased to note that no one paid him particular attention.

He then visited one of the two general stores to pick up some essential supplies, including a new rifle, a revolver and some ammunition to replace those left behind at the scene of the hanging. He stuck with the popular 1873 Winchester, which his father had taught him to use and which he felt comfortable with. He figured its 400 yards range would more than meet his needs, especially as he could use the same ammunition as the Colt .45 Frontier six-shooter the store's owner recommended. Fortunately he had more than sufficient money to meet his immediate needs.

Rory and his father had been taking a short midday rest when David Pritchard and the ranch hand Ned had caught up with them. They had been surprised to see that they had been followed, and assumed that the two arrivals were bringing some sort of news from the family ranch. It had been easy for Pritchard and his hired hand to disarm the father and son by the simple act of holding a rifle to Rory's head and ordering the pair to discard their weapons. But they had not got round to taking the money from Jack Rimmer's saddle-bag.

'We're taking you back to face trial for stealin' from us,' David Pritchard had told Rory's father.

'Don't be stupid,' Jack had replied. 'All I took was money that is rightfully mine. For twenty years I've given you and your lousy brothers much more value than you've ever given me credit for. I've worked my boots off on that ranch and you've hardly given me more than food on the table. I'm entitled to the money Ann and I had saved.'

Angrily, David Pritchard squared up to his brother-in-law. 'We've given you and your son a roof over your heads. What more could a no-good drifter expect? You came in and sweet-talked my sister into gettin' married to you and settled in as if you had a right to be there. Now she's dead you think you're just gonna leave without us doin' anything about it. Well, you're wrong. You're goin' back to face the music. We ain't gonna let you just ride away when you feel like it.'

'You ain't takin' me and Rory anywhere.' Instinctively, Jack Rimmer stood and raised his fists as he confronted Pritchard, who responded by swinging a mighty punch. For minutes the two exchanged blows, with Ned keeping Rory at gunpoint so that he could not intervene. In the end David Pritchard landed a stinging sledgehammer of a blow to send his opponent reeling to the ground. Before Jack Rimmer could recover, Pritchard grabbed a rifle and brought the butt down on the back of his head, knocking him unconscious.

Sweating profusely, Pritchard turned to Ned. 'Tie 'em both up and gag them,' he ordered. 'I'm gonna string this bastard up.'

Ned had protested: 'We can't just hang him. The law is bound to catch up with us.' But he was angrily ordered to do as he was told.

'Just get on with it,' said his boss.

CHAPTER EIGHT

When Rory returned to the stable after his visit to the store, he immediately appreciated the well-groomed appearance of his mount, and of the two other horses in the girl's care. She obviously didn't waste time and wasn't afraid of a bit of hard work.

'Looks good,' he complimented her.

'Lovely animal,' she responded. 'You sure you don't want me to ride him a bit this afternoon?' she asked, almost pleaded.

'No, not today, I told you,' Rory replied gruffly, but then, seeing her hurt and disappointed look, softened the harshness in his voice. 'Perhaps tomorrow,' he added.

'Will you still be here?' she questioned. 'Thought you might be taking off.'

'No, I'll stay one more day,' Rory replied, immediately regretting that he had given her more precise information than he considered wise. By way of explanation, he added: 'Gonna get myself a bath and a haircut before I set off. I'll settle up with your boss tomorrow night and take off at daybreak the next day.'

'OK, mister. You'll probably find me here. I'm usually with the horses. I like 'em better than most people,' she added quietly.

As it happened, it was a good decision to stay an extra day, because Rory was in no fit state to ride out the next morning. His head throbbed and his stomach felt as if a horse had kicked it. Either the eating-house he had used was not up to scratch, or his body was reacting to over-indulgence after the near starvation of the cross-country ride from the scene of the hanging.

By the time Rory felt fit enough to leave the Moontime Hotel, the day was well advanced, with the sun already high in the sky. When he went to the stable the girl was not there. Neither was his horse. Rory cursed to himself and hoped she wasn't working the animal too hard.

A couple of hours later, Rory returned. This time the girl was back and he was pleased to see his horse was not sweated up.

'I just took him down to the creek and let him stand in the shade by the water,' the girl said. 'He's a lovely animal.'

'Sure,' grumbled Rory. 'He should be. He comes from good stock.'

'I love horses,' said the girl. 'My pa has only got the one left and Big Blue – that's what I call 'im – is getting a bit old now. But the stable owner lets me take others out, so I get to ride quite a few mounts.

42

I'm a pretty good horsewoman,' she added with shy modesty.

Somewhat won over by her natural enthusiasm, Rory relaxed a little and sat down opposite her. 'What's your name, girl?'

'Julie. What's yours?'

Rory hesitated a moment, then recalled the name he had given the stable owner and the hotel clerk. It was a little confusing when you changed the name you had lived with for nineteen years.

'Wilson,' he said. 'Tex Wilson.'

'Well, Mr Wilson, are you still plannin' on leaving tomorrow?'

'Yes. Early. . . .'

'I'll be here,' she said. 'I'll have him ready for you.'

'Don't your ma and pa mind you spending so much time here?' asked Rory.

She smiled. 'No. My ma's dead and as long as I do my chores, Pa don't mind me coming here and working for Mr Jackson. There ain't much else to do around this town. Besides, you said you might give me an extra tip,' she added with a laugh.

'OK, Julie, we'll see.' He got up to leave, but realized he really had nothing he needed to do. Instead, he just stretched himself a little and was pleased to find that he now felt much better. The girl watched him, without speaking. He sat down again and looked at her more closely. She was slim, even for her age, with ginger hair left loose and somewhat untidy around a cheerful face with a sprinkling of freckles.

'How long you been livin' in Bush Creek?'

'Pretty well my whole damn life,' she said in a voice that made her short lifetime sound like a couple of centuries of tedious existence.

'We came here when I was five and my mother died of consumption when I was eleven, so I have to look after Pa and the house and sometimes help him when he's doin' a job for someone. But he don't bother much now. We ain't got much money, but we get by with my earnings and what we get from the chickens and the eggs. Pa has sold off the three good horses we had.'

'Ain't you got a fella?' Rory was surprised to find himself asking.

'No, not me. There ain't many young ones in town, and anyways I fell out with them when I used to go to school. Useless, most of 'em.'

She laughed gently, not a young girl's giggle, but an appealing gentle ripple of sound. 'There was one,' she added. 'But when he got to sixteen he had a fight with his pa about him wanting to be a doctor. His old man said he shouldn't have such big ideas.'

She paused, recalling the incident as if it had taken place many years ago. 'His pa told Jim to be a ranch hand like his brother. They argued about it for ages. In the end Jim just rode out one day, without tellin' anyone – not even me. We ain't seen 'im since. That was two summers back.' She paused again, deep in thought, then added: 'That's what I should do.'

Her words ended in an upward inflection, suggesting a question or seeking Rory's approval of her desire to leave Bush Creek, but he declined to comment. He didn't regard it as any of his business whether she stayed or left, even though he had a sneaking sympathy for her position. She was obviously an intelligent young thing, with a rebellious streak which, he guessed, would not long allow her to continue what she clearly regarded as a monotonous existence in this unexciting small town.

'Where you headin', mister?' she asked.

'You ask too many damn questions,' he replied, though the initial roughness had now left his voice. 'Besides, I ain't entirely sure I even know.'

'Then if you don't know where you're goin', then I guess you're wanting to get away *from* something,' Julie hazarded. 'Just like me.'

'No, not just like you,' Rory replied, carefully choosing his words, so as not to reveal more than he wanted. He clammed up, but Julie cleverly switched the subject of conversation.

'I hear you had a run-in with our town marshal, Tiny Whiney,' she said.

Rory smiled at the cruel but clever nickname. 'That what you call him?'

'Yeah, but only when he can't hear us. No one really knows what to think of him, or knows much about him. He rode in about a year or so ago and asked to see the marshal. When he was told we didn't have one at that time, he simply announced that he thought he should have the job. The adults talked about it a bit and then decided that no troublemaker was likely to argue with a bulk of a man like him, so they appointed him. I think they got it agreed officially later on. Anyway, he moved straight into the marshal's office, which has got a bunk-room as well as an office and a cell, and he's been here ever since. He don't mix with other folks much, but since he became marshal we ain't had no trouble in town, 'cept for a coupla fellas gettin' drunk sometimes. So I expect he'll stay as our lawman for as long as he wants. His real name is Mason but the kids in school started callin' him Tiny Whiney and some of the adults do too, but we all call him Marshal Mason to his face. Everyone's a bit scared of him, I think, 'cause of his looks.'

'Yeah, I know what you mean. He sure scared the wits out of me and I won't be sorry to get out of his sight tomorrow. So I'll see you in the mornin' ... early.' Rory gave his horse a couple of gentle slaps, and turned as if to leave. But, after three or four steps, he stopped, walked back to the girl and held out coins he had been holding in his hand.

'Guess you've earned these,' he said, 'but perhaps I should wait until the mornin' before I give them to you.'

Recognizing that she was being teased, Julie returned his smile. 'Yes,' she agreed, 'maybe you should wait and see how much you've got left when you've paid for your room.'

CHAPTER NINE

As he rode out of town, Rory gave only a casual glance over his shoulder. He guessed that – if they were pursuing him – the Pritchard brothers would already have made their presence felt in town, or would now wait until they had ridden well clear of Bush Creek before making a move to challenge him.

Nevertheless, as he rode out further across the open countryside that lay outside the town, he had an uncomfortable premonition that he was not alone.

After about twenty minutes' steady, but not forced, riding he turned off the trail towards a small bluff and pulled his mount into a boulder-strewn area where he had a good view of the land he had just crossed. Sure enough, over to the left, a few hundred yards away, there was a small dust cloud that indicated another rider, or riders, approaching the outcrop with the intention of riding round the other side of it. Carefully Rory circled round the far side himself and hid away in a position where he would be

47

able to see who was approaching.

From his vantage point it soon became apparent that it was only one rider. At least that was a relief! He was sure that the two Pritchard brothers would come after him together, possibly bringing an experienced tracker and one or two ranch hands along, too.

When the rider drew within rifle range, Rory fired a single warning shot and yelled: 'Hold up there, stranger. Let's see who you are.'

As his shout echoed back from the escarpment, the lone rider pulled to a halt whilst scanning the rocky outcrop to try to locate where the shouted challenge had come from.

'Come closer, but slowly,' commanded Rory, less nervous now as he became fairly sure he recognized the owner of that distinctive copper hair poking out from under a flat-crowned hat with a strap under her chin. 'What the hell you doin'?' he shouted. 'Why you followin' me?'

'Can I come in closer and talk properly? I don't mean you no harm,' came the reply.

'As if you could,' shouted Rory. 'Well, what *do* you want?'

'I was hoping you would let me ride with you a while.'

'Why?'

Her reply was muted, so Rory couldn't hear her properly. 'OK. Come in,' he shouted.

'What the hell are you doin' out here?' he demanded again as she rode closer.

'I wanna ride with you. I won't be a burden. I just

have to get away from Bush Creek.'

'Of course you'll be a helluva burden. I've got some hard ridin' to do and—'

'I can ride just as hard as any man,' she butted in. 'And I've got a good horse.'

'Yep. I can see that, but he don't look like no old Big Blue to me. Where did you get him from?'

'From the livery stable.'

'Great – so you're a horse-thief,' groaned Rory. 'And what provisions you got? Food? Water? And I can't see no gun.'

'I can look after myself,' said Julie, defensively. 'I got enough stuff to last three days. I don't eat much. And I've got a gun hidden away.'

'Get down off that horse,' Rory ordered. 'And come to this side of the rocks.'

As she moved round, Rory carefully scanned the horizon behind them.

Noticing, she dared to ask: 'Are you ridin' from someone, rather than something?'

'More likely someone will be ridin' after you,' he replied angrily. 'Stealin' a horse ain't a joking matter.'

'Don't think so,' she replied. 'The old fella what owned it ain't gonna come far in this direction in the hope of gettin' his horse back. And I didn't take any of his tackle, or saddle or anythin'. And I left a note, to say to give the earnings Mr Jackson owes me to the owner. Mr Jackson has been saving some of my money so that my pa didn't know I had it. There was quite a bit.'

'Well I hope he pays up,' grunted Rory, 'though I doubt that you left enough money for a horse like that.' He paused. 'Now let's have something to eat and push on. I want to cover a lot more ground before we stop tonight.'

Julie turned away to hide the huge grin on her face as she realized that – without him actually saying so – Rory had accepted that he would be letting her ride with him. 'He ain't turnin' me back,' she whispered to herself, as she dismounted.

They stopped for only a very short while for a drink and a little food before Rory ordered that they should ride on. He deliberately rode a bit faster than he knew they needed to, in order to test the girl and her mount. It was soon clear, however, that both were more than capable of keeping up, and would not hinder Rory in his flight. Her horse was, like Rory's, a strong animal but had more distinctive markings – a prominent nose flash and white forelegs contrasting with its dark overall colouring.

When they made camp that night Julie tried to get Rory into conversation, but he remained morose and uncommunicative. He was thinking through his options.

Despite her protestations, it was still possible that the owner of her stolen horse would pursue them, but Julie seemed confident that he posed no serious threat. Besides, what difference would one more possible pursuer make if the Pritchard brothers were indeed on his trail?

On the other hand, she was good security cover.

The men who might be trailing him would not be asking about a man and a girl when they made their enquiries in any towns or homesteads they might stop at. But the more he chewed it all over in his mind, the more Rory had to admit that there was one other factor to take into account: he liked the idea of having her with him. The trail was going to be lonely and it felt good to have her along, even if they had so far talked little because of his reticence.

As they drank their coffees before bedding down, Julie tried again to draw him into conversation. First, she talked about her own life. She told how her father had withdrawn into himself after the death of her mother, and paid little attention to Julie or her progress – or her problems. He had never asked about her schooling and responded without real interest when she had tried to tell him about what she was learning from Miss Green, the town's solitary teacher. She was a spinster in her fifties who struggled bravely to deal with the complexities of her pupils' widely diverse age groups, limited abilities and lack of interest in anything beyond their own immediate horizons. She loved it when, just occasionally, she came across a bright pupil like Julie who was eager to learn.

Theirs was a small town which had developed as a staging post for the cattlemen and early settlers, but now it was in decline as the railway up to the north had left Bush Creek stranded.

Julie tried to convey to Rory some of her excited interest in the world outside, but received little feedback, as her new companion remained reluctant to reveal anything about his own background. His own private thoughts were still very much occupied with his father's death, and his own unplanned but fateful step into a world of extreme violence.

He was uncertain about the future, knowing that he had now irrevocably cut himself off from his previous existence. He admitted to himself how much he grieved for his dead parents, but acknowledged that there was now no way he could return to the lush Eastern valley and wooded territory he had left behind but still thought of fondly.

CHAPTER TEN

They rode steadily throughout the next day, without pushing their mounts too hard. The landscape was changing now as they steadily progressed west, with wider stretches of grassland interspersed with occasional trees and brush.

In late afternoon, as the hot sun started to sink towards the horizon, they saw a small stone-and-adobe building ahead of them. As they approached, they were espied by a sturdy young boy of perhaps five or six years of age, who disappeared round the side of the building, shouting as he went.

Rory and the girl approached slowly. They dismounted and Rory called out: 'Hi, folks.'

For a couple of minutes, their greeting brought forth no response. They hesitated, wary of approaching the doorway without being invited.

'Shall we go in closer?' queried Julie.

'Best not,' Rory replied. 'I should think folk can get a might touchy about strangers when they are stuck out here in the wilds. The boy was obviously calling out to someone, so we'll let them set the pace.'

As they waited he was wary enough to remain ready for any kind of hostile response. His hands rested by his sides so that they were clearly visible, but he knew that he could have his right hand on his Colt in a second if need be. As well as giving his son a good general education, Jack Rimmer had been assiduous in teaching Rory what he termed 'the rudiments of life', by which he meant shooting, fishing and hunting.

After a couple more minutes of unnerving silence, Rory was just about to shift his position when a husky female voice called out: 'Vat you want? Who is you?' As she spoke, a short, plump woman wearing a shapeless gingham dress came from round the side of the building. In her hands was an old European rifle of a kind Rory hadn't previously seen, but by the way the woman held it, he had little doubt that she knew how to handle it and wouldn't hesitate to do so if necessary.

'Two strangers passing through,' he replied.

'We mean you no danger,' added Julie.

The sound of a female voice seemed to give the woman confidence. Still holding the rifle firmly pointed forward, she advanced a few steps. She studied the visitors closely for a minute or so further, then seemed to relax.

'How far haf you come?' she asked in her guttural accent.

'Been ridin' all day,' replied Julie, sensing that the

woman would be more at ease if she took the lead.
'We sure would welcome it if we could bed down
somewhere for the night and maybe buy some food
from you.'

As she spoke the boy who had first spotted them
reappeared and stood behind the woman. He asked
a question which neither Rory nor the girl understood. But his appearance and question seemed to
soften the woman's attitude. She lowered the rifle
and let her natural hospitality take command.

'Best put your horses round back, in the shade,'
she suggested. 'There's water and hay.'

A while later the four of them were seated inside
the homestead, which was more advanced in con-
struction than many of the scarce homes in the area,
and obviously built by a skilled carpenter with some
style touches that indicated a European background.

The woman had served up a simple meal based on
wild turkey and vegetables grown on the plot of land
to one side of the building.

Once relaxed and obviously appreciative of having
some rare company, she explained that, with her
husband and son, she had arrived at this spot a year
ago. Like others in this area, they were Germans who
had finally settled here after twice moving further
west, having originally landed at Galveston to escape
from religious persecution in their homeland. As
they talked, Rory gently got round to the question he
had been puzzling over since they had arrived. At last
he asked, as casually as he could manage: 'Where's
your husband now?'

Suspicious of the motives behind the question, the woman hesitated before answering. Nervously she then revealed that he had ridden to get supplies from the main town of Bladenheim, not far up north of where they were.

Whilst they had been eating and talking the boy had several times gone to look outside, had returned with a worried look, and twice asked his mother – in German – the same question that Rory had posed. She had tried to reassure her son, but failed to hide her own worries at her husband's absence. Now she decided that she could confide in the two strangers sharing her basic repast.

With obvious concern she revealed that her husband was long overdue. She had expected him back the previous evening. Now it was getting dark again and he had still not returned. She was fearful because there had recently been talk of Western cattlemen chasing off homesteaders who had started to settle on what the ranchers considered to be their own grazing lands.

Eventually she decided that they should wait no longer. She cleared up the few pans, told her son, Boris, to go to bed, and indicated where Rory and Julie should sleep on the floor.

CHAPTER ELEVEN

As dawn broke the next morning, Rory awoke with a start. After the long ride he had slept soundly, despite the unfamiliar surroundings, but he was now aware of movement inside the dwelling and the noise of horses outside.

As he rose Julie was also stirring beside him. At the same instant, he saw the German woman standing at the open door with her rifle at the ready. She shouted a question but as she did so a shot came from outside and she slumped backwards, dropping the rifle as she fell.

The boy had appeared behind Rory and started to move round him to reach his mother, but Rory roughly pushed him aside and moved towards the open doorway himself. As he did so, two more shots came from outside, with one nicking the young German boy on the shoulder. He screamed and dropped to the floor.

Rory looked carefully round the edge of the door-opening and saw two riders turning their mounts away from the building.

They were clearly Mexicans, perhaps renegades still unprepared to accept that the so-called Mexican War, promulgated by President Polk way back in 1846-48, should have brought a decisive end to Mexico's claims on Texas territory. Or perhaps they were simply bandits, with no higher motive than personal gain.

Rory was unconcerned about the attackers' status, however. Without hesitation he fired off a shot with the Winchester he had left standing by the edge of the doorway overnight. His bullet hit one of the attackers in the middle of his back. He fell instantly to the ground, and stayed motionless while his mount carried on. Rory allowed himself a moment of self-satisfaction at his success with his new, but familiar, weapon.

When he saw that the second rider had reached the protection of a large thicket, Rory waited several minutes. Then, hearing no sound, he walked over to inspect the body about fifteen yards from the homestead. Warily, he bent over the prostrate form, but it needed little inspection to assure him that the man was indeed dead. He removed his guns and, still facing towards the thicket with his rifle at the ready, walked carefully backwards to the open doorway of the building.

From the sounds he had heard he was fairly convinced there had only been two attackers, so his main concern was to ensure that the one who had ridden off had really departed. He told Julie to keep a good lookout from the front window space, whilst he inspected the German woman.

'Is she dead?' asked Julie.

'Sure is.'

His blunt response brought forth a pitiful whimpering from the boy, who was now crouched in the corner of the room and obviously spoke enough English to understand. Rory stared at him, but made no comment. Instead, he moved the woman's body clear of the doorway, then moved into the back room where the three members of the German family had slept. He unbolted the window shutter and peered outside. There was clear ground for about twenty yards, before the start of the broken line of thicket which curved around the building and joined the cover into which the Mexican had disappeared. Rory went back to Julie. 'Seen any movement?'

'No, nothin' at all.'

'Keep a good watch,' he told her. 'I'm goin' out the back window, to work my way round to where that Mexican disappeared. We can't be certain he isn't just sittin' there waitin' for us to leave.'

Julie looked alarmed. 'But what about me and the boy?'

'Just keep your eyes and ears open. If anything happens, you'll probably hear.'

Julie immediately understood that he was indicating the possibility that he might not return safely. 'You take care, Tex,' she said, as Rory made his way into the back room and then eased out of the window. As soon as he dropped to the ground, he sprinted for the cover of the thicket behind the dwelling. Once there, he rested and listened, but could hear nothing. After a few minutes he started to work his way cautiously and somewhat painfully through the rough growth that went round that side of the building.

He stopped frequently to listen for sounds, but heard nothing. Eventually he was level with the place where the rider had disappeared through a gap in the thicket. After pausing again he pushed further into the undergrowth. Suddenly his body stiffened and nervous sweat trickled down his back as he heard voices. He stealthily worked his way closer to the sound, and was able to discern the bright-red cape that had been on the back of the Mexican he had seen earlier. He couldn't see anyone else, but the sound of low conversation confirmed that at least one other person was present.

With extreme care, Rory climbed a few feet up the branches of one of the larger trees. The extra height enabled him to confirm that there were only two Mexicans. They sat talking together animatedly.

Nervous, but knowing that he had the advantage of surprise, Rory levelled his rifle and called out loudly. 'Raise your hands, *now*! Pronto.'

Immediately, the Mexican facing him pulled out his revolver and fired in Rory's direction. He was clearly shooting blind, and did not realize that his intended target was not at ground level.

With his warning ignored, Rory had no choice. He knew that if he didn't shoot, then he would certainly be writing his own death warrant. He first fired at the man who had shot at him, and was gratified to hear him scream and see him fall sideways to the ground.

As he toppled over, the Mexican made a vain attempt to pull himself back up, but he collapsed in slow motion, almost as if in a drunken stupor. As he hit the ground, his companion turned, stood up and raised his rifle. He clearly was not about to surrender either, as his eyes searched for Rory's location. But he was too slow. Rory's carefully aimed shot hit him full in the chest and the man's whole body shook with the impact of the bullet. For a moment he stood his ground and Rory was tempted to fire another shot. As he took aim, however, the Mexican buckled at the knees and his body slowly slipped face forward on to the ground.

Perhaps wise beyond his years, Rory remained on his perch for a full three minutes to make sure there was no movement coming from either of the Mexicans or anyone else who might be near by. When satisfied, he clambered down, moved cautiously round a couple of bushes and carefully approached the two bodies. He first reached the man in the red cape. The bullet had hit him close to the heart and there was little doubt he was dead.

Still cautious, Rory stepped round him to inspect the second man, who was slumped forward. With his Colt to the man's head, Rory pulled him into a semi-sitting position. He was still alive, but was clutching both hands to his wound, vainly trying to stem the flow of blood. The Mexican looked up into Rory's face. There was terror in his eyes as he tried to speak. It sounded like '*Por favor. . . .*' but that was all he was able to manage. The attempt at speech turned into a choking gurgle before the man's head fell sideways. He, too, was dead.

For long moments, Rory was frozen into inaction. Sickened by his father's brutal and senseless death, he now acknowledged the shocking reality that – without even reaching his twentieth birthday – he had himself already become a multiple killer. Unplanned, he had created a tally of death that would surely see him committed to hell when his time came. The recognition filled him with remorse, but as he stared at the two lifeless forms on the ground before him he could feel only limited personal compassion for them as individuals. They were strangers and their response to his offer of surrender had been to shoot at him. His own reaction had been automatic, with no conscious premeditation, but that did not assuage the feelings of sadness and guilt that now enveloped him as he acknowledged that he had taken two more human lives.

CHAPTER TWELVE

'Tex, I was so scared,' said Julie as he re-entered the homestead.

'Don't call me Tex. Call me Rory.'

Julie looked at him with surprise, but the grim tone of his voice persuaded her not to pursue the matter now. She didn't even question him about what had happened outside. She had heard the three shots and feared the worst, but he had returned unharmed and that was all that mattered. The questions and explanations could come later.

Her thoughts turned instead to the young German boy. Although the random shot from the raiders had caused only a minor flesh wound, Boris was now screaming as if he had been mortally injured. Eventually the girl managed to calm him down after they had bandaged the wound, but Rory was deeply concerned with the dilemma he now faced.

His priority was to dig a shallow grave for the dead German woman but, as he laboured, he could think of no obvious way to resolve the problem of what to do with Boris. He had already determined in his own mind that he was not prepared to stay longer at the homestead in the hope that the father would return. The reason for the man's failure to appear was unknown, but there was no cause to hang around on the vague chance that he would still show up.

For one moment, Rory considered leaving Julie with the boy and riding on alone, but he quickly dismissed that idea as he reluctantly admitted to himself that he had really become too involved with her to simply desert her – even if she would allow him to.

Though not usually averse to making his own decisions, he found himself consulting with her about their most effective plan of action. Julie was vehement that they could not leave the boy alone. She stood with her arm protectively around him in an effort to console him. 'We must take Boris to that town the woman said her husband had gone to. She said it was only a couple of hours away.'

So, after packing a few things on to the Mexicans' animals, they set off along the rough trail. They had hardly been riding for fifteen minutes before they saw, just off the trail, a small wagon with the horse that had been pulling it tied up to a tree a few feet away. As they approached cautiously Rory saw a leg sticking out from behind the wagon's wheel. Still hesitant, he called out: 'Come out from behind there. I've got you covered.'

With no response or movement forthcoming, Rory carefully circled round to where he could see that the boot he had spotted was attached to a body, and there was no doubt the body was a dead one – shot several times, including once right in the face.

There was no problem with identification, however, since the boy's whimpering made it clear that the dead man was his missing father.

Clearly the three bandit Mexicans had been responsible and were probably intending to return here after raiding the nearby homestead. So, after Rory had hitched the nearby horse back to its wagon, the party of four – including the dead body – continued towards Bladenheim.

With the boy still whimpering, Rory and the girl moved in silence through the land of gentle contours, where scattered trees stood within the shallow valleys. It was a forgiving terrain and, after only a couple of hours' steady riding, they reached the outskirts of what was clearly a growing and prosperous town. There was excitement in Julie's eyes but concern in Rory's thoughts. He was more than a little apprehensive at what developments might now take place, when they rode in with a dead body and a lot of explaining to do.

CHAPTER THIRTEEN

As they entered the town's wide main street, Julie's excitement increased. She looked with amazement at the square, solid houses of quarried stone, with bold staircases leading up to attics. 'Look at those stores,' she screeched. 'And those buggies. Aren't they grand? And the clothes! I've never seen women dressed like that. Wow!'

She didn't have long to take in the sights, however. They were soon surrounded by a group of German-speaking residents who obviously recognized the boy, the wagon and – when they peered inside – the dead man who had been a fairly regular visitor. It was immediately clear that this was another place where, as in Bush Creek, Rory would not get away with remaining an anonymous stranger. Anyone following him and asking questions would soon find out about the blond youngster with the chestnut horse, even though he now had a girl and a young boy in tow.

Within minutes everything was organized. Two women had quickly taken the boy under their wings and marched him off somewhere. The wagon and its contents were led away, together with their horses, and the newcomers were shepherded into what was clearly the new extension to a house which was being developed into an inn.

Soon they were seated at a sturdy oak table and brought a substantial meal of beef and fresh vegetables. They were not allowed to eat it undisturbed, however. After only a few minutes, four men came to the house and were ushered into where Rory and Julie were eating.

A tall man, speaking in English but with an obvious Irish accent, led the questioning. He wanted to know what had happened at the homestead, and there was much excited comment when Rory explained about the Mexicans. From the exchange of comments, mostly in German, it was clear that incidents of this kind were not entirely unknown.

Yet the Irishman then indicated to Rory that the townspeople had feared that perhaps the attack had been the start of the kind of cowmen's reprisals against nesters that they had heard had been taking place further into the plains. They seemed almost relieved that the attackers had been what they termed 'only Mexicans', and appeared not too disturbed that they had been killed.

However, the questioning then centred on Rory and the girl. Who were they? Where were they from? Where were they heading?

As the girl started to reply, Rory unsubtly kicked her leg under the table and gave her a brief but ferocious stare, which clearly told her to keep her mouth shut. With his careful reticence, Rory managed to answer the men's basic questions without giving too much away. Though he never actually said so, he conveyed the impression that he and Julie were a married couple. He said simply that they were 'riding West' to settle down when they found somewhere that suited them.

'If you are going West, keep your eyes skinned. We've been warned there's a small bunch of hostiles around who didn't go up to Oklahoma with the others. They are in a pretty desperate state, so be careful,' warned the group's spokesman, much to Julie's obvious horror. After a little more questioning, the couple were shown up to a comfortably furnished bedroom with ornate fittings and luxurious curtaining that caused Julie to exclaim with delight how beautiful everything was. Either side of the central window were two single beds. As Julie continued examining the room Rory quickly pulled off his boots and pants and wordlessly clambered into the luxury of the soft bed.

His tiredness immediately relaxed his body, but his mind was again a whirl of unbidden thoughts. Recollections of the traumatic events of that morning mixed with tender thoughts of his dead mother. And intermingled with these contrasting images was the constant fear that he was almost certainly being pursued by the vengeful Pritchard brothers.

Despite his physical tiredness, Rory accepted that

sleep would probably not come easily – especially when a new dimension was added to his mind's complexities. He was resting on his back with his eyes closed, when he felt soft hair touching his face and somewhat less soft lips pressed against his own.

'Sleep well, dear Rory,' said Julie's voice before she crossed to the other bed and jumped into it, leaving her companion with an entirely different set of thoughts and emotions to contend with.

The next morning Rory was dismayed when the Irishman and two others reappeared and said the town councillors wanted him and the girl to ride back with their county sheriff to the scene of the previous day's raid on the homestead.

Vehemently Rory refused, proclaiming volubly that he and the girl had nothing to answer for. 'We killed the raiders in self-defence,' he argued. 'They had already shot the woman and injured the boy, and would have done for us too if I hadn't gotten them first.'

The argument went back and forth for a full ten minutes or so, with Rory getting increasingly agitated. Julie feared he was about to strike one of the men, but he eventually calmed down when the Irishman said quietly, but forcefully: 'We've got your horses, and you ain't leaving until we say so. We just want to check that everything was like you said it was.'

Seeing that he was outmanoeuvred, Rory suddenly capitulated, though his red face and the set of his jaw showed that he was still deeply angry at having to return the way they had come the previous day.

'OK,' he said. 'But we go *now.*'

So, within twenty minutes, Rory and the girl found themselves being escorted back along the same rough trail that they had traversed the day before.

As they neared the homestead they pointed out where they had found the wagon and the German's body. One of the four men who were acting as their escort carefully studied the markings on the ground and confirmed that three horsemen had indeed been involved in the killing. They then continued on to what they called the Metzner home, where they spent an inordinate amount of time inspecting everything in minute detail and questioning Rory and the girl about exactly what had happened. They made Rory retrace his route through the thicket to the place where he had killed the second and third Mexicans. Two of the men set about burying the bodies on a site well away from where Rory had respectfully buried Frau Metzner.

At last the Irishman who had done most of the questioning and talking indicated that they were satisfied, and they should now all ride back into Bladenheim.

Rory practically exploded.

'No way,' he shouted. 'We ain't goin' back into town.'

'What you afraid of?' the Irishman asked. 'We just want to ask you some more questions, and make sure everything is recorded and dealt with properly.'

'We ain't goin' back,' Rory repeated angrily. This time he reinforced his oral statement with the simple physical act of drawing his Colt and pointing it at the oldest of the men from the town. Immediately, the sheriff, who had been standing slightly to the side, also withdrew his gun from its holster and pointed it at Julie. They all stood silently for what seemed an age, with no one ready to break the stalemate.

Eventually the man looking down the barrel of Rory's gun gave a rueful smile. Although he hadn't said much, this man seemed to be deferred to by the others, as though holding some kind of authority. He was perhaps sixty years old and was still dressed in European-style clothing rather than the more practical Texas-style dress favoured by the others. His only concession to the fiercer Texan conditions was a wide-brimmed hat, which he now slowly doffed in a conciliatory manner.

He spoke to the sheriff in German, clearly indicating that they should not force the two strangers to stay if that was not their wish.

'We will not detain you,' he said with only a slight remaining trace of a European accent. 'Now please put your gun away.'

Rory thought for a moment, and decided to trust the man's word. He silently returned his Colt to its holster, and the sheriff followed suit.

The four Bladenheim men then collected a few small personal belongings from inside the homestead and, with wishes of 'God speed your journey and protect you,' they set off back to town.

Rory, too, prepared to leave but found to his amazement that he had another argument to contend with.

'I think we should stay here tonight and set off early in the morning,' said the girl, in a voice that displayed a determination Rory instinctively knew he would not easily overcome. He argued, but his resistance was only a token one. He again briefly considered simply leaving the girl behind, but instantly knew that was not an option he would choose to adopt, and not only because of the obvious danger that that would leave her in.

They ate a simple meal from the provisions they had brought from Bush Creek, supplemented by a few vegetables from the Metzner plot and coffee prepared on the stove Rory had lit earlier. As they then started to settle down for the night, the girl half-undressed. She looked at him pointedly, then asked: 'Are you goin' to do it to me?'

'Do what?' asked Rory somewhat naïvely, though the way she was looking at him made it quite obvious what she meant.

'You know,' she said. 'What men do to their women.'

'But you ain't my woman.'

'I could be, if you wanted.'

'I ain't a safe man to be with,' Rory replied. His words were few, but contained a mixture of emotions – fear, anger, and a sense of desperation.

'What are you runnin' away from?' the girl asked gently. 'Perhaps you had better tell me about it.'

72

And, to her surprise, he did, but not until after they had made love in the not over-comfortable bed in which the ill-fated Metzner couple had lain only four nights previously.

For both of them it was their first full sexual experience. Hesitantly, Rory entered her and was amazed by her eagerness after an initial first gasp of pain as her virginity was taken. Unable to contain himself, he then pumped into her with an energy and passion which not only met his physical needs but also – at least momentarily – removed his emotional anxieties.

When they had both worked themselves to satisfied exhaustion, Julie kissed him again and murmured: 'Now I really am your woman.'

CHAPTER FOURTEEN

As Rory and Julie lay side by side after their coupling, he painfully started to explain the events that had led to them being together in this isolated farmstead.

He spoke slowly and deliberately, using it as an opportunity to get a clearer understanding in his own mind of the memories and feelings that had been bottled up inside him. He was speaking to himself as much as confiding in the girl. 'You ought to know I killed a man,' he started.

'I know. There were three of them. I was there,' she acknowledged.

'No – not the Mexicans. Before that. I stabbed a man with his own knife. It was easy; the knife went into him so smoothly. It hardly took any effort.'

Rory paused, as the memory and horror of that so-recent day came back as a vivid picture in his mind. Then, with anger in his voice, he added: 'He deserved it. He hanged my pa, and I had to watch!'

'He hanged your pa?' There was shock in Julie's voice. 'Why?'

Still trying to understand for himself why anyone should take another man's life in such a callous manner, Rory hesitated.

'He was my uncle,' he eventually continued. Rory paused again, thinking back to his own childhood.

'We lived on a ranch, but my pa didn't never have a share in it. My uncles said he was just a driftin' man at heart, and I suppose they were right, really. But he drifted into the ranch where Ma lived with her brothers and just stayed. He stayed because he wanted to be with her. He loved her; truly loved her. But the three brothers, my uncles, never really wanted him there. They saw it as their ranch, started by their own father, and they weren't about to share it – not even with my own ma's chosen partner. They said he wasn't proper kin, and always treated my pa as an outsider. He worked hard, but they never let him share in any of the decisions. They resented him bein' there, and treated him like a ranch-hand rather than like my ma's husband. She once told me they didn't want her to marry him, and two of them didn't even bother to go to the wedding.

'Two of them – Frank and Jake – had their own wives and two children each, all girls, but it was never like I was their kin. The others went off to school, but I was taught by my ma and pa. And the others never let me join in their games or nothin'.'

He paused again. The remembered exclusion still hurt.

'You wanna' hear more?' he asked.

'Yes, of course,' Julie replied. 'I want to know all about you. Or, at least, whatever you're happy tellin' me,' she added, remembering his earlier reticence and not wishing to push him too hard.

'Well,' he continued after further hesitation, 'I guess we never was all a proper family – not all of us. Pa was always on at Ma to move on. He wanted to ride south and start up on his own, but Ma always said the time wasn't right. She said we would be wrong to take the chance when we already had a good home and regular food on the table. But I remember Pa saying: "It may be *your* home, but it sure ain't mine. Those brothers of yours won't never let it be my home. And I think it will be the same for little Rory." '

'Is that really your name?'

Rory suddenly laughed. 'That's me,' he said.

'But you told me your name was Tex Wilson,' she exclaimed. 'Was you lying to me?'

'Afraid so, but you must understand I had to be careful. I reckon they'll be after me.'

'Who?'

'My other two uncles – Jake and Frank – and maybe a couple of ranch hands too. Ned would have ridden back to tell them what I had done to their brother David. They would have soon set out behind me. They never took to me anyways, so now will be their chance to get me. Like they got my poor pa.'

'But why did they want to kill him?' Julie dared ask.

'They reckoned he had caused Ma's death. But it

weren't really like that. He wanted her to come away with him. He asked her, and asked her. They argued for three nights in a row, with my ma doin' lots of pleadin' and sobbin'. In the end, Pa lost his temper. It was the only time I saw him do it. He pushed Ma away from him and she fell and hit her head. She had bruises she couldn't hide and so her brothers knew something had happened. They had heard the argument but Ma said she had slipped and it wasn't serious. The brothers made her go to the doctor. He examined her and told her to go to bed and rest for a couple of days, but that night when my father went to the room he found she had died.'

Rory paused, his emotion stopping his flow of words. When he recovered his composure he told Julie that, two days after the funeral, there had been the fistfight he had been forced to witness.

'The brothers grabbed my pa and beat him pretty hard. It was like Ma's death was the excuse they had been waiting for. David started it after an argument with my pa. He called my father a wife-beater. They fought for quite a while, with Jake joining in as well. Pa held his own against the two of them for ages. I was real proud of him. But eventually they beat him to the ground, and it took me quite a while to bring him round.'

The shock and hurt was clear in Rory's voice, and he again took a while before he continued his narrative.

'After Ma's funeral Pa decided it really was time to leave and told me I had to go with him. "There's

nothin' here for you, Rory. You're coming with me,"
he said.'

Rory explained to Julie that he had not been sure
that he wanted to leave, but acknowledged that –
except for his mother's grave – there was indeed
nothing to keep him there. His father was right.

'So we rode out together, thinking that was it. But
we was only two days out when my Uncle David and
one of the ranch-hands jumped us in camp. Uncle
David ranted and ranted at my pa. He went on and
on about my pa being a worthless drifter who had
killed Ma. They fought again until David knocked Pa
unconscious with a rifle. Then he said he was goin' to
string him up.'

He paused again, still recalling the horror.

'At first Ned didn't want to do it. He said they
should take us back, but David wouldn't have it and
ordered Ned to do what he was told. And they did it,
with me forced to watch them.'

Rory's story skipped some of the details of the slow
and painful hanging, even though his mind was filled
with the image of his father left dangling on the end
of the rope after his horse had stepped away.

'Pa's body was still hanging there,' he continued.
'He gave a few last twitches, and a sort of gurgling
noise came from him before he finally fell silent.
Before that I could tell he was desperately tryin' to
say something to me, but they had tied his bandanna
round his mouth, so I just couldn't make out what he
was tryin' to say.

'He repeated one phrase over and over, but I still

couldn't understand. I think now it might have been "Forgive me". Eventually, when my father's body had stopped movin', my uncle's ranch-hand Ned got up from the log they were sittin' on. He went over to Pa, pushed his feet and made him swing. It was horrible. Then my Uncle David came over and started to untie me. . . .'

At this point, Rory stopped his narrative. 'I had better explain that my uncles weren't actually my uncles in a direct sort of way – though my ma always said I should call 'em that,' he continued.

'They was my ma's brothers, all right, but they had a different father from her. Their pa died young. My ma's mother married again, then had my ma as a baby several years younger than the three boys. The brothers never took to my grandpa, their new step-father, but he and Grandma both died in a stupid buggy accident soon after my ma was born, so the brothers looked after her and cared for her as she grew up. I think that they were kinda jealous when my pa came along and she fell in love with him. It was like he took Ma away from them. I think that's really why David strung 'im up in the end. Don't make much sense, though.'

Rory's thoughts returned to the day of the hanging, and his voice took on a sort of detached tone as he continued his story, telling Julie about the way he stabbed his uncle, his escape from Ned Pointing and his ride to Bush Creek, where he thought to take on the false name Tex Wilson in case he was being followed.

'I was scared, real scared. Still am, I suppose.'

Rory stopped, stunned by his own vivid memories. Then he let out a groan and said, more to himself than to the girl: 'I left Pa hangin' there. I just left him hangin' there.'

Julie, beside him, reached out and put her arms around him, and he reciprocated. They stayed like that, silent for a long while, until Rory simply ended his story by saying: 'I'm sure they'll follow me.'

The two of them stayed side by side, silently, without closer intimacy, until eventually the girl fell asleep and he followed soon after.

CHAPTER FIFTEEN

The next morning, Rory Rimmer woke with a start. Outside the homestead he heard a man shouting, followed by two shots.

'Come on out of there, Wilson,' yelled the voice. 'We know you're there. Come out with your hands held high.'

'What is it about this place?' Rory asked the girl as she woke and came to stand by him at the side of the small window. 'Every damn mornin' you're wakened by someone shootin' at you.'

'Who is it?' asked Julie. 'Is it your uncles?'

'I didn't recognize the voice,' Rory replied, 'but it couldn't have been one of them or he would have used my real name. Tex Wilson was the name I used in Bush Creek.'

'Of course,' Julie agreed. 'That's the name you told me.'

Another shot came from outside, followed by a different voice.

'Come on out, fella. And bring my daughter with

you, you rotten woman-stealer and horse-thief.'

'I'll be . . .' Julie started. 'That's my pa.'

'Come on out,' repeated the first voice, 'or else we'll start shootin' for real.'

Rory turned to Julie. 'Guess we ain't got no choice. There's no way we can get out of here without shootin' them dead, and there ain't no way I'm gonna start firing lead at your pa.'

Once outside, they were quickly surrounded by five men, including Marshal Mason and Julie's scrawny father, who made a show of giving the girl an elaborate parental hug. Julie was slim, but her father was nothing more than bones with a thin, parched covering of skin.

'What he do to you, girl?' asked this live skeleton.

'Nothin', Pa,' she assured him. 'He didn't do nothin'. I chose to go with him. I followed him out of Bush Creek myself.'

'What?' her father exploded. 'You mean you just took off after a stranger without even tellin' me?'

'I did tell you,' she replied. 'I left a note.'

'Note? What note? I didn't see no note.'

Before Julie could elaborate, one of the other men cut in angrily. 'Be that as it might. Don't alter the fact that he's a no-good horse-thief,' he accused, stabbing his finger into Rory's chest as he did so. 'Ought to be strung up for that, regardless of what he did to the girl.'

'But he didn't do nothin' to me, I told you,' insisted Julie. 'And it was me that took your horse, Mr Penney.'

As the argument and accusations continued, Marshal Mason cut in, using the authority of his badge to determine the course of action.

'I reckon all this is for the judge to hear,' he said. 'So let's get something to eat in the shack and then head back to Bush Creek. And no funny business from you, young fella. You're my prisoner and you're gonna stand trial for stealin' a horse and a girl. And I reckon you've got some real explainin' to do about the new graves over yonder. Looks to me like there's been a whole heap of trouble round this place afore we caught up with you. My guess is you've been a bit too useful with that gun of yours, so you can hand it over right now.'

During the ride back to Bush Creek, Rory tried in vain to persuade the marshal that he was in no way responsible for abducting the girl or stealing the horse, but found himself in deeper trouble when he tried to explain what had happened at the homestead. His admission that he killed the three Mexicans was seized upon by the lawman as evidence that he had caught a real gunman, even though he himself considered that killing Mexicans was not in the same league as stealing a horse. The marshal had killed quite a few in his time. Nevertheless, he felt secure that the convictions surely coming the youngster's way would undoubtedly safeguard his own continued monthly payments as Bush Creek's law officer.

Privately he knew that it was his pure good fortune that Rory had been so easy to capture without a struggle when, following a fairly cold trail, they had hit upon the Metzner homestead and the owner of Julie's mount immediately recognized his distinctive horse tied up outside.

With the youngster offering no resistance to his capture, the whole exercise had gone extremely satisfactorily and the marshal was a very happy man. Expecting the town's plaudits for tracking down and capturing a gunman capable of committing such a variety of wrongdoings, the marshal eagerly looked forward to the forthcoming trial.

As they continued the ride back, Julie continued to try, in vain, to persuade her father and other members of the posse that neither of them was guilty of any crime.

In particular, she vigorously tried to assure her father that Rory had not abducted her and that it was she – not he – who had taken the horse she was now riding. 'I explained it all in the note I left for you on the table,' she told him repeatedly, but her father simply replied that he hadn't seen a note and, anyway, she knew he would have struggled to make any sense of it.

'You tryin' to make me look stupid?' he asked. 'You know I have trouble with words. But there weren't no note.'

'But Pa,' Julie insisted, 'I knew you could get Miss Green or someone to read it with you. I didn't just ride off without tryin' to tell you why. And no one forced me to go. I just followed . . . him.' She realized just in time that she had nearly used Rory's real name, and made a firm mental note that, as far as Bush Creek was concerned, he was still Tex Wilson.

She tried to explain to her father why she had wanted to get away but her words failed to impress him.

'There ain't nothin' wrong with Bush Creek,' he insisted. 'It was good enough for your poor ma – God rest her soul – so it ought to be good enough for you. No reason for you to take off like that unless you was made to.'

Rory's attempts to persuade the marshal that he was making a mistake were equally unsuccessful. All he got from Tiny Whiney was the unpromising assertion that it wasn't for him to decide. 'My job is to lock you up, young fella, and the judge's job is to decide what to do with you. I warned you we don't like trouble in our town, but you rode off with a girl and a horse and heaven knows what else you got up to. The place for you is behind bars.'

CHAPTER SIXTEEN

The nature of their arrival in Bush Creek took Rory and Julie by surprise. One of the posse had gone ahead and it seemed that the whole town had turned out to see them ride in.

Marshal Mason was in front of the small group. Rory Rimmer was roped to him, with his wrists tied crosswise on his saddle horn. Clearly the marshal was intent on showing that the young gunman was his personal captive and the town should be grateful that it had such a successful lawman.

Julie rode next, alongside her father, with the other two remaining posse members behind.

The reception was noisy, with people talking excitedly to each other and pointing to the young captive as an item of unbounded notoriety. One or two shouted comments such as, 'Well done, marshal', and Mason's ugly countenance softened as he smiled in acknowledgement of their praise.

When they reached the marshal's office Rory was hastily locked in the cell, but then the marshal came back out and seemed uncertain what to do with Julie. She had, after all, claimed that it was she – not her companion – who had taken the horse, but it didn't seem prudent to the marshal to lock her up with his male captive in the single cell. In the end he told Julie's father to take her back home.

'But be sure she don't do another disappearing act. We want her for the trial.'

In fact, it was five weeks before the circuit judge arrived. He had been summoned to preside over the trial of a young fella who had perhaps committed a whole string of crimes – abducting a young girl; stealing a horse; killing Mexicans; and maybe gunning down innocent homesteaders as well.

This sounded like a trial that would attract a lot of attention, and Judge Gordon Jennings was not averse to that. He was building a reputation as someone to be respected for his thoroughness and, when required, his willingness not to shirk from the ultimate sentence of a legal hanging.

Word had spread, though, that he was also a compassionate man. In the town of Santana they had built a gallows in the knowledge that a man who had publicly admitted to killing his wife would almost certainly be strung up.

The basic evidence was clear, but Judge Jennings had kept encouraging the defence lawyer to question witnesses until it became evident that the woman had several times been unfaithful to her husband with a neighbour. Lurid tales were told of them being interrupted during naked intercourse in a barn, and even of the couple staying at her home for their unlawful coupling while the husband was at church.

Furthermore, there was the clear admission by the wretched husband that he had been pushed too far, and he had retaliated by doing his own pushing: tipping his wife into a well. There could be no disputing that he was guilty and a hanging was the undoubted outcome. To everyone's surprise, however, the judge directed the jury to find that the killing had been justified and he ruled that the husband should be released.

The relieved man could hardly believe his good fortune and rode out of town the next day while his luck lasted.

The townsfolk kept the gallows standing, though. They were regarded as a good warning to any potential wrongdoers.

For Rory the long wait for the judge's arrival was a torture in itself. He had first ridden into Bush Creek looking over his shoulder and determined not to be there for more than a couple of nights. Now, weeks later, he was back, with no prospect of escape – either from Marshal Mason or, if they were indeed on his trail, from his mother's brothers.

Rory didn't know what to make of his prospects on either front. He knew he was innocent of the accusations for which he was currently locked up, but was far from convinced that he would be found not guilty.

With regard to the vengeful Pritchards, he was

even less certain what to think. He had no doubt in his mind that, when the ranch-hand Ned reported back to them, David's two brothers would have been determined to seek out their sister's son. But he had ridden hard and they would have had no idea where he was heading.

By the time Ned had returned to the ranch and they had set out after him, the trail would already have been cold and difficult to pick up, even if they had employed an extremely skilful tracker. Perhaps by now they would have given up the search. Or perhaps they were still scouting out in all directions, asking questions and seeking clues as to his whereabouts or at least his direction of travel. If that were the case, it was inevitable that, sooner or later, they would arrive in Bush Creek. And if that happened they would certainly have no trouble finding out where he was, even though Marshal Mason's prisoner was still identified under the alias he had used when first arriving in the township.

The *desperado* known to Bush Creek as Tex Wilson would soon come to the attention of anyone asking questions about a young stranger who had recently arrived in the town. In that case, the false identity would provide no cover, and would perhaps even be seen as a further indication of his guilt. Innocent men did not need to travel under false names.

So Rory's period in jail was one of constant fretting. Whichever way he considered his position, the future looked bleak.

There were, however, a couple of redeeming features of his incarceration.

At first Julie's father had kept her in the house, refusing even to let her resume her previous duties in the livery stable. After a while, however, he relented and she presented herself to Marshal Mason to plead Rory's innocence and ask to be allowed to speak with him.

Again, the immediate reaction was a refusal, but – like her father – the marshal found her persistence impossible to resist. At first she was allowed only a brief talk with the prisoner and to bring him extra food to supplement his somewhat meagre official rations. When no harm seemed to come from these meetings, however, the marshal relented further and more or less allowed Julie to visit as much as she liked, much to the prisoner's delight.

He found her visits more than just welcome breaks in the monotony. She was a real pleasure to talk to and her continued insistence that everything would turn out well almost persuaded him that there was some hope.

'Of course it will be OK,' she insisted. 'They've got to believe me that you didn't do anything wrong. How can they say you stole me away when I say you didn't?'

Her logic and persistence were appealing. Despite his basic pessimism, Rory felt encouraged that her testimony might be sufficient to persuade the jury, despite the town's inherent belief that the young stranger must be guilty of something. Why else would he have been riding alone? And hadn't they seen him tangle with their marshal on his first night in town?

Julie's encouragement turned into something more solid, however, when she came excitedly to him one morning during his third week in jail.

'A messenger has come from Bladenheim,' she informed him breathlessly. 'The marshal sent for word of what happened at the Metzner homestead, and now Tom Kane has brought a big letter package for Tiny Whiney.'

'What does it say?' Rory asked her anxiously.

'I don't know. I asked the marshal and he just said I had to wait and see. He didn't seem none too pleased about it, though.'

Together they speculated for nearly an hour on what might be in the package. The marshal had gone out so they were able to talk freely through the bars that divided them, but their physical separation had become lessened by the fact that they now sat holding hands. The marshal had seen them doing it earlier and looked disapprovingly but had said nothing.

Now, in his absence, Julie put her face to the bars and whispered: 'Kiss me, Rory.'

He did so and in that moment he acknowledged to himself just how much she meant to him. His feelings increased his developing resolve to prove himself innocent, but would the package from Bladenheim help his case?

Long though they debated it, Julie and Rory were

unable to come to a conclusion. The threat of the gallows remained all too real.

CHAPTER
SEVENTEEN

For the people of Bush Creek, the trial was to be a major event. Judge Jennings had decreed that, in the absence of any other suitable location, the Lucky Horseshoe saloon was to be used as a substitute courthouse. This decision, of course, caused considerable consternation – not only from the owner but from his customers, too.

After some debate, a compromise was reached. The saloon would have to double up as a courtroom, but only between 9.30 each morning and noon, when the furniture could be quickly rearranged and the premises reinstated for their less formal purposes. For the morning sessions it was arranged that the judge would be seated on a platform, with steps, which was erected behind the bar. This had the bizarre effect of giving him a huge mirror and rows of bottles and drinking vessels as a backdrop, but Judge Jennings quickly established the serious purposes to which the morning was devoted when he opened the proceedings.

'Some of you,' he said to the packed assembly before him, 'will have frequented these premises for a variety of pleasures. I want it clearly understood, however, that whilst I am sat here this is a court of law, and I expect it to be given the full respect that is due to it and the proceedings that will take place here.'

He paused, to let his words sink in and perhaps to see whether there would be any inappropriate behavioural response or ribald comments. Reassured, however, by the respectful silence and the eager expectancy that pervaded the room, he continued in an educated accent indicating that he originated from somewhere up north or east, perhaps Carolina.

'The accusations made are of a most serious nature, and could result in a premature end to a young man's life.' As he made this comment, he looked straight at Rory Rimmer so that no one could be in doubt as to whose life was under threat.

For Rory himself, the judge's words had a chilling effect. It sounded almost as if a judgment had already been reached and all that remained was the jury's formal ratification before the hangman's rope received its victim. He scrutinized the judge carefully but could divine nothing further from his countenance or manner. Although of only slight build, the judge carried with him an air of authority well suited to his appointed role, or perhaps even shaped by it.

He was around fifty years of age, with sharp facial features and a slightly receding hairline which had the effect of making his forehead look as if it sloped immediately back from above his thin eyebrows. Inappropriately, Rory found himself thinking that the distinctive pointed nose looked like the beak of an equatorial parrot he had once seen in a neighbour's home. It took an effort of will for Rory to stop his daydreaming and bring himself back to the proceedings that would determine his future, if indeed he had one.

The judge allowed the young and very nervous defence lawyer to start the main proceedings by calling Marshal Mason to give evidence, initially by describing events immediately following the defendant's arrival in Bush Creek. The marshal testified that, from enquiries he had made, Tex Wilson had arrived alone and stabled his horse before checking into the Moontime Hotel.

'These details,' he said as pompously as his squeaky voice would allow, 'could be confirmed by the hotel clerk, Señor Vasquez, and the livery owner, Mr Jackson.'

The marshal then asserted, without this time giving the names of his informants, that the young stranger had subsequently been seen talking at length, and with apparent intimacy, with the girl, Julie Denham.

'Did you yourself have any contact with the accused man?' interrupted the judge, impatient with the lawyer's slow presentation.

'I did indeed,' the marshal confirmed. 'It was in this room.' He hesitated, then added: 'When it was being used for its more normal purposes.' This comment, which was delivered with a slight smile, brought forth a muted titter of laughter from around the room, but this break in dignified behaviour was immediately silenced by a stern look of clear disapproval from the judge.

The marshal continued: 'He was sat drinking *in my chair* when I arrived. I asked him what he was doin' in town, and I thought he was gonna draw on me.'

'Did he, in fact, do so?'

'No sir,' replied the marshal, without further elaboration, but additional information came from a shout delivered from the back of the room: 'He didn't have a gun!'

The judge's eyes searched the room, but he was unable to identify anyone to receive directly the rebuke that was conveyed by his angry glare. Instead he turned back to the marshal.

'Is that true?' he asked.

'Yes, but I wasn't to know that, was I?'

'In future,' admonished the judge, 'make sure you don't leave out relevant evidence.'

Suitably abashed, the marshal then responded to further questioning in a relatively straightforward manner. He recounted how Julie's father had reported that she had gone missing, and that a horse had also been stolen from the stable the morning the accused man had left town. No one had actually seen him leave, however, so it wasn't possible to be sure he had taken what the marshal pompously described as 'the two relevant items of property'.

He then reported how he had immediately formed a posse – 'Just a *small* one, Judge' – and set out to track down the accused man and the missing girl.

His testimony was basically factual, with only slight exaggerations and embellishments designed to accentuate the firm leadership role and determined action taken by the marshal himself. He described in detail how they had tracked the couple to the Metzner homestead, even making it clear that tracking marks showed that to begin with the couple had followed different routes out of town.

The significance of this was not missed by his listeners, but the defence lawyer made it transparently clear by asking the marshal to confirm that the girl could not possibly have been taken out of town forcibly if they hadn't even ridden together.

At this point most eyes turned to Julie's father, who for weeks had been proclaiming loudly to anyone who would listen: 'My poor girl was stolen from me by that evil man. Heaven only knows what he put her through.'

Even when it came to the description of the actual surrender of the accused man, the marshal resisted the temptation to overstate the difficulty of the capture. There were, after all, other posse members who might contradict the veracity of his description if he made the event sound more heroic than it actually was. He did manage to make clear, though, that this time the fugitive was indeed armed and potentially dangerous.

'We had to holler and shout before he came out and surrendered his rifle and his revolver,' said the marshal.

Surprisingly, the assembled listeners managed to suppress any amusement they might have felt at the idea of it being Tiny Whiney's squeaky voice that had done the hollering. The combined effect of the marshal's glare and the judge's well-established authority proved to be a strong deterrent to any inappropriate behaviour.

Somewhat to the marshal's chagrin he was stopped in full flow when he was starting to describe the return to Bush Creek. The ornate clock above the bar where the judge sat indicated that it was noon, and there was a pronounced restlessness in the room from those who realized just how dry their throats had become.

True to his word, Judge Jennings immediately brought the session to a close by dismissing Marshal Mason with the perhaps unnecessary order that the accused man should be returned to his cell.

'Proceedings will resume promptly at 9.30 tomorrow,' concluded the judge, leaving the townsfolk ample time to refresh themselves and also to go about their daily business and debate at length the guilt or innocence of the man on trial.

On the second morning Marshal Mason was given the opportunity to resume his description of how he had brought the accused man and the girl back to town.

When questioned by Rory's lawyer, who was gradually becoming more confident, the marshal grudgingly admitted that the captive had caused no trouble, either by trying to escape or in any other way.

'The girl, though, was a pest,' he added. 'Wouldn't stop talking all the time, sayin' as how it was her what took the horse and how she rode out after him of her own choice.'

He was stopped at this point by the judge, who indicated that he wanted the jury to hear from the girl at first hand. Excitedly, but lucidly, she described how it was entirely her decision to follow Rory – though she was careful to use his assumed name. 'He didn't even suggest it, and certainly didn't force me,' she proclaimed.

'Then why did you go?'

Julie blushed bright red at this, so that the reason was clear despite her inability to put her feelings into appropriate words. Still blushing, she looked at Rory and whispered: 'I just wanted to.'

Realizing he was going to get nothing further from the embarrassed girl on that score, the prosecuting lawyer moved on to the question of the horse.

'What horse did you ride out on?'

Julie hesitated, and then admitted that she had taken one from the stable. She explained that it had been lodged there by a local homesteader, who had been sick and was staying in town while he tried to recover.

'It's quite a strong and wilful animal, and I

thought Mr Penney might not be wanting it in future, seeing as how he was sick,' she rationalized. 'I couldn't take my own because he's just too old. But I left money to pay Mr Penney. I left a note for Pa to give him my savings and my earnings from Mr Jackson – everything I've got.'

'Where did you leave the note for your pa?'

'On the table. He must have found it. But he says he didn't,' she admitted.

The makeshift courtroom fell silent as everyone took in the importance of what she had said, and the significance of the missing note. Without evidence of the intended payment, young Julie Denham was convicted out of her own mouth of the heinous crime of horse-theft. It was she, not the accused man, who now faced the force of the law on that particular accusation.

CHAPTER EIGHTEEN

For a few moments after Julie's admission of horse-theft, there was silence in the room as the audience contemplated her evidence.

The judge started making some notes on paper which was resting on his makeshift bench, and as he did so the silence ended as everyone started talking to those around them. The noise volume rose, and Judge Jennings hammered on his bench as he ordered silence. The chatter mostly subsided, except that there was a special commotion to one side.

The judge again called for silence, but as the general noise level reduced an excited male voice called out: 'Look! Her pa's got the note. He's got it. He's got it.'

This time, it took a full three minutes for the judge to regain control of his courtroom. Everyone was straining to see Julie's pa, old Paul Denham, who was now standing and waving a sheet of paper.

'Bring that here,' ordered the judge, and a passage was gradually formed so that Julie's father could approach the judge and hand over the paper.

A slightly more muted hubbub continued as the judge carefully flattened the crumpled paper and privately read its contents. He looked down at the man who now stood before him, head hung low and shoulders slumped.

'How long have you had this?' the judge asked.

'Since Julie rode out.'

'Why didn't you produce it before?'

Denham hesitated, before simply replying: 'I guess I forgot.'

'You forgot? Something this important, and you forgot!'

'Well, sort of.' The humiliated man seemed to sink into the wooden floor in the face of the judge's obvious anger and disbelief. In a hardly audible voice, he added: 'I was mad at Julie for going. Some of her things were missing, so I knowed she had gone, but I couldn't properly make out the words. I don't read too good, Judge.'

Again hubbub ensued as those at the front of the room relayed the gist of Denham's quietly spoken admission.

The judge had had enough.

'I'm closing this hearing for today,' he said.

He turned to Marshal Mason. 'Take the girl and her pa back to their house for the night and don't let either of them out until they are brought back here tomorrow morning,' he ordered. 'And put him back in the cell,' he added, pointing at Rory. 'We haven't finished with him yet. There's still the matter of the murders to deal with.'

As Julie and her father were taken out of the saloon by the marshal, two of the posse members were told to take Rory to his cell.

His mind was in turmoil. He reckoned that Julie's evidence and her father's production of the note might clear him of the charges of abduction and horse-theft, but the judge's final words made it clear that the accusations of alleged murder were still standing. Throughout the afternoon and the long night he considered his position, and worried about Julie.

If the letter her father had produced was accepted by the jury as genuinely written before her departure from Bush Creek, then it was possible that her position was improved. However, the fact remained that she had taken the horse without its owner's permission, and that still constituted horse-theft even though she claimed that she had left payment behind. Try as he might, Rory could not convince himself that the jury would be prepared to accept that as a sufficient extenuating circumstance to remove her guilt.

So, as he drifted at last into a troubled sleep that night, his concerns were more for Julie's plight than his own. He could only view the following morning with the utmost apprehension.

Day three of the courtroom hearings was delayed somewhat because of a general commotion. It seemed that everyone in town wanted to get inside the converted saloon. Even the marshal had trouble getting Julie and her father in through the crowded doorway, and he had to use his considerable bulk to force an entrance.

Eventually, stern words from the judge and physical pressure from the marshal prevailed, though the room was crowded to an unbearable degree.

To their amazement, however, it turned out that the trial was all over very speedily. Dealing first with the matter of the alleged abduction, Judge Jennings said he was convinced from the marshal's evidence and Julie's own version of events that she had left Bush Creek alone and of her own free will. 'So I strongly recommend the jury to find Tex Wilson not guilty of abduction,' he said in his most solemn voice, 'and it is clear that he didn't steal the horse, either. So on both these charges you should find him not guilty!'

Untutored in the ways of the law, and naturally respectful of the judge's commanding recommendation, the jury took only a few minutes' deliberation to indicate that they agreed. As he heard their verdict, relief flooded through Rory as he realized he had been cleared without even being required to give any evidence himself.

His joy was to be short-lived, however. Calling again for silence, Judge Jennings continued: 'The other charges will be dealt with in a separate trial starting tomorrow morning.' It was not over yet for Rory Rimmer.

Similarly, Judge Jennings dealt speedily with Julie's

crime. Addressing the apprehensive girl, he said: 'You have been foolish, and very impetuous, as well as a cruel and thoughtless daughter.

'However, I have shown your note to the horse's owner and told him about the amount of money you had saved and had owing to you by the stable owner, and he says he is prepared to accept this as sufficient payment, rather than have his horse back. The poor man is in a bad way and is not fit to give evidence in this court. The posse ride did his health no good at all and the doc says he may not live long, so he wants the money to go to his wife.

'In the circumstances, I am prepared to accept that you acted in haste and did not really intend to cheat the owner of the animal. As he is willing to accept your payment, we'll regard the transaction as a legitimate sale. Therefore the accusation of horse-theft is not valid. You are free to go.'

So Julie's name was cleared, but for Rory a second trial awaited and this time Marshal Mason, feeling somewhat thwarted by developments so far, refused Julie's request to speak with his prisoner.

Back in his cell, Rory was left to fret on his own. As the evening's low sun cut through the bars and formed a grim pattern on the wall, his concerns remained in two directions. Whilst he had to cope with the strain of the trial, his mind was still also constantly attacked by thoughts of his father's killing and the danger from his uncles. Time was passing, and it was perhaps inevitable that their search would eventually bring them to Bush Creek. In many ways the threat of their likely thirst for vengeance was more worrying than the proceedings in the courthouse.

CHAPTER NINETEEN

For Rory's second trial in Bush Creek there was less public interest. The saloon was only half-full, as most people took the view that it was no particular concern of theirs whether or not the young stranger had killed some people they had never met and didn't particularly care about.

It was only those with nothing much better to do who bothered to turn up. The rest were prepared to wait for the hanging that would surely follow if the accused man were to be found guilty of murder.

The proceedings started with Marshal Mason being asked to repeat part of the evidence he had given at the earlier trial, when he reported finding four fresh graves outside the Metzner homestead. He confirmed that, on one side, he had found a tidy grave which carried a neat wooden cross carrying only the name *Mrs Metzner* on it.

Away from the small homestead there were three further graves, carrying insignificant marker boards with no names.

'When I took Julie to the graves,' said the marshal, 'she told me that the young fella – sorry, Judge, I mean the accused – had only dug one for Mrs Metzner. She said the three graves for the Mexicans were dug by the townsfolk.'

'Did she tell you who had done the killing?' asked the prosecuting lawyer, who felt on safe ground in building his case.

'Yes she did. She said the Mexicans killed the wife and then Wilson killed them!'

At this point Rory was suddenly tempted to interrupt, as he felt a strong desire to give his real name rather than force Julie into using his alias. Now that he had been declared innocent of the earlier accusations, he felt a need to put the record straight, but just as he was about to speak, he realized that that would entail explaining why he had used a false name in the first place.

As he turned it over in his mind, he noted that the judge had finished with the marshal. Now, for the first time, Rory was asked to give his own version of events.

Without referring to the reason for his arrival in Bush Creek, he straightforwardly described his first talks with Julie, and his surprise when she followed him out of town.

Almost without interruption he was allowed to relate the whole of the rest of the story, right through to his capture by the marshal and enforced return to Bush Creek. The jury and other listeners were particularly attentive when he described the Mexicans' attack on the homestead and his subsequent killing of the two in the woods. Except for a few coughs, and a little cheer of approval at the description of the final killing, the room remained remarkably quiet throughout the testimony.

At the end of Rory's story of the events and a brief summing-up from the two lawyers, the judge produced a sheaf of papers and addressed the assembly.

'These papers,' he said, 'have been sent to me from Bladenheim. They tell how the sheriff there carried out an investigation of the whole matter. He took particular evidence from the Metzners' son, who is now being looked after in the town.

'The papers confirm what we have heard in this court this morning. The good folk of Bladenheim have now buried the boy's father next to his mother at the homestead.

'They consider that the man before us now acted quite properly, indeed bravely, in all the circumstances. The Mexicans were clearly those who had been causing trouble in the area for some time and the sheriff says he is quite happy to accept that they were killed in self-defence. The town's council say Julie Denham and the prisoner acted commendably in taking the boy and his father's body into town and no blame is attached to them.

'In view of these papers and the evidence we have heard, I conclude that there is no case to answer and I am therefore declaring these proceedings closed.'

Rory Rimmer had safely come through his second trial at Bush Creek. As far as the law was concerned, he was a free man. Only he and Julie knew of the other threat still hanging over him.

At the swift conclusion of the second court hearing, Julie screamed with delight and pushed her way over to Rory to throw her arms round him. Although embarrassed by her public show of affection, he was equally overwhelmed to find himself being patted on the back and congratulated by those around him.

It seemed that his reputation had undergone a complete reversal in the minds of the townsfolk. From being considered at first as some kind of desperado who had ridden into town and stolen a girl and a horse, he was now transformed into a hero who had removed three troublesome bandits, gained the respect of the people of Bladenheim and – most important – won the affection of the town's young Julie.

Even Julie's pa, old man Denham, came and shook his hand. 'What you gonna do now, young fella?' he asked.

Rory was uncertain, still not knowing whether he was being pursued by the Pritchard brothers.

'Better come and stay with us,' Julie's father offered, much to her surprise and delight.

With no other plan in place, Rory accepted and within a few days was ensconced as a new citizen of Bush Creek. He and Julie visited the sick man, Mr Penney, to thank him for his part in cancelling the charge of horse-theft. A few hours later the man died and they subsequently attended his funeral, along with many of the town's population.

Normally few of the townsfolk or those on the scattered homesteads would have bothered to turn out, but the events of the trial had stimulated some kind of new community spirit and anyone connected with the trials was the subject of enhanced public interest. So it was that poor Mr Penney was blessed with many more mourners, or at least interested spectators, than his death would normally have warranted.

After the funeral his widow approached Rory and asked whether, if he was staying in town, he would consider helping at her homestead while she sorted things out. She seemed delighted when, after little hesitation, he agreed.

Life seemed to have taken some surprising turns but Rory was constantly conscious of the danger he was in. Part of him still clung to the idea that he ought to ride on.

On the other hand, despite the nightmares he still suffered over the events of his father's hanging, he found himself drawn to the hope that the Pritchard brothers were not, after all, seeking him out and that he might be safe to stay in this somewhat isolated township, where he now appeared to be unreservedly welcome.

Even Marshal Mason seemingly carried no major disapproval of the 'not guilty' rulings over someone once judged by popular opinion to have been a major threat to society. He was secretly pleasantly surprised that his part in the capture and his prominent role in the resultant two trials seemed to have softened people's attitude towards him.

He knew his pure physical presence would continue to gain him their respect, but now more people seemed to treat him as a less distant figure, using cheery street greetings rather than formal ones. He even found some of the children openly addressing him as Marshal Tiny – but without the adjective "Whiney" – when they passed him by. In fact, Marshal Mason felt more at ease with himself now than he could recall in many previous years.

CHAPTER TWENTY

Two weeks after the trials had ended, Rory had not taken any positive action to leave Bush Creek.

He had helped the widow, Mrs Penney, run and maintain the small homestead while she prepared to hand it over to a neighbour so that she could move into town, where she intended to start a small bakery business. He had also assisted Julie's father with some building maintenance work, which in some cases had long been promised but never actually achieved.

Julie herself was delighted at the effect Rory's presence seemed to have had on her father. 'I've not seen Pa so content and energetic since Ma died,' she said. 'He really seems to have got back his interest in living. He even said he was pleased I hadn't gone away. Before I took off after you I don't think he even noticed whether I was there or not, as long as the chores got done.'

'So what would happen if I rode out of town again? Would you follow me again?'

'You know I would. If you wanted me.'

'Yes, I want you,' said Rory as he embraced her and sought her lips.

He knew now that he could not leave Bush Creek alone, fearful though he still was that the two Pritchard brothers might show up to avenge their brother David's death. But an incident was to occur that would further cement Rory's growing ties to the town.

Early one morning he was mending a fence for Mrs Penney when he heard her voice raised in an argument with someone. With the hammer still in his hand, Rory walked round the side of a barn to find that a man he had not seen before had arrived in a fancy buggy and now faced Mrs Penney with his hands gripping her shoulders and his face pushed threateningly close to hers.

'You will sell to me,' he shouted, 'otherwise you could find some very unpleasant things happening.'

'No, no,' protested the woman. 'I've promised it to Mr Pollock and we've agreed a fair price.'

As she spoke the stranger shook her violently. Rory rushed forward.

'Help me, Tex,' called Mrs Penney as she spotted him approaching.

Her attacker wheeled round to face Rory, speedily drawing his revolver as he did so. 'Drop that hammer,' he ordered as he spotted the tool in Rory's hand.

Rory stood his ground. 'And if I don't, are you gonna shoot me in cold blood? And perhaps kill Mrs

Penney as well? Do you really want to hang?'

The man hesitated, undecided what to do.

Behind him, Mrs Penney – though obviously scared – added her own threat. 'If you do anything silly, everyone will know it was you, John Gibson. The whole town knows you tried to get my husband to sell this place cheaply to you when he first fell ill, and they'll know it was you now, so put that gun away.'

The man half-turned towards her, and away from Rory. As he did so, Rory leapt forward and deftly brought the hammer down on the man's revolver. The gun fell to the ground. The enraged Gibson snarled and threw himself at Rory. He was a large man, and with considerable strength he got Rory in a bear hug so that the hammer he still held was a useless weapon.

In this position they struggled for many seconds before the man managed to push a breathless Rory backwards so that he fell with his assailant on top of him. The man then moved his hands in an attempt to get a grip on Rory's throat, but as he twisted to do so Rory slipped from beneath his weighty bulk and gave him a hefty kick on the shin.

Still on the ground, Gibson tried to grab Rory's legs as he scrambled to his feet. Rory evaded his grasp but the hammer was still trapped under his opponent's body. There could be little doubt that Gibson, with his natural physical advantage and with the hammer as a weapon, would be more than a match for Rory as their battle continued. But as Gibson started to rise, and Rory fearfully prepared to defend himself, Mrs Penney saved the situation. She had picked up Gibson's dropped revolver and now handed it to a very relieved Rory. He gratefully seized the initiative.

'Leave that hammer where it is and get up slowly,' he ordered. Gibson obeyed, but his face was contorted in anger and frustration. 'Now get back in that fancy rig of yours and ride out. And don't come back. We'll be reporting this to Marshal Mason, so no doubt you can expect a visit from him.'

Sullenly, Gibson climbed into his buggy, but before driving off he turned again to Rory. 'You no-good interfering bastard,' he snarled. 'You ain't seen the last of me. You can bet on that, so watch out.'

In fact, when Rory and Mrs Penney went into town, the excited widow didn't just report the incident to the marshal. She told everyone she laid her eyes on, and even went visiting a few acquaintances to tell them what had happened and how the brave young Tex Wilson had been her saviour. Charitably, she chose not to mention that it was she who had picked up the dropped Colt and handed it to Rory.

Word quickly passed from person to person and in the eyes of the folk of Bush Creek, Rory (or Tex Wilson, as they still knew him) was soon established as a hero figure to be admired and respected.

For Rory, however, staying in Bush Creek was still a cause for constant concern and fear, and these nagging worries were brought forcefully to the surface a week later when a breathless Julie came running up to him. 'Rory, I think they've come. Little

Johnny Butler has just told me that two men have ridden into town, and are asking for the marshal. It might be your uncles, come looking for you.'

Rory pondered for a minute. Escape seemed impossible, especially if he was to take Julie with him. Even if they were to get out of town quickly enough, with fresh tracks to follow the brothers would undoubtedly soon catch them.

Equally, staying where he was would do no good. They would speedily locate him, especially if they were even now asking the marshal where they could find him.

No, the best option was for him to go to them, he decided. If they were still with the marshal they would hardly gun him down in the sight of the town's lawman. Perhaps, thought Rory, I'll get a chance to explain my side of the story.

So, despite Julie's protests, he buckled on his Colt and headed swiftly to the marshal's office. As he turned the corner towards it, the two hitched horses outside made it clear that the two strangers were still inside, but Rory didn't recognize either of the mounts as belonging to the Pritchard brothers.

As quietly as he could, he stepped on to the board-walk, passed the closed door of the marshal's office and went up to the open window. He paused to listen, but did not recognize the voice he could hear inside.

'We been waitin' a long time for this, Mason. Pure chance we run into a fella' in a saloon who was tellin' a tale about a big man with a small voice.'

'It had to be you fittin' a description like that,' growled a second man. 'So we asked him a little more and he told us about Bush Creek. Scruff of a town, he said. Run down after the railroad took a path north and left this place with no purpose. Seems fittin' that a no-good like you would end up in a no-good place like this.'

'Sad place to die, though,' continued the first voice Rory had heard. 'Make no mistake, that's what we're here for. They're gonna find you dead in your own cell, mighty Marshal Mason. Now get in there.'

'Ain't you even gonna give me a fair chance?' Rory heard the marshal ask.

'What chance did you give us when you got us locked up for six lousy years?'

'You two didn't deserve no chances. Guilty as hell, the pair of you. You had a fair trial.'

'Maybe, but we would never have been caught if it hadn't been for you tracking us down, you stinkin' bounty hunter. Shocking what a man will do for dollars. Now get in that cell.'

Hearing movement inside, Rory waited a few seconds, drew his gun and then burst through the door. Inside, he saw one of the strangers holding open the interior door through to where the cell was. He was pushing the marshal through to the back. The other man was by the office desk, with his back to Rory. He spun round, reaching towards his revolver as he did so.

At such close range, Rory was able to be extremely accurate with his shot. He fired at the nearest stranger's shooting arm and was rewarded with a yell of pain as the bullet shattered his elbow and continued on to embed itself in the office wall.

At the same time Marshal Mason turned and grappled with the other man, who had been distracted by Rory's entry. The marshal grabbed the man's gun hand with his own left and delivered a mighty punch with his right as he did so. The two of them crashed through the middle door towards the cell area, and passed out of Rory's sight.

Rory moved towards the man he had already shot, who was now desperately struggling to use his unharmed left hand to remove the gun still in the holster on his right side.

'Hold it, mister,' Rory warned, his own Colt still pointed at the man. 'Or I'll shoot again.'

The warning went unheeded, however, as the man gave up the effort to draw his gun, but instead grabbed the edge of the table. With surprising determination, considering his damaged arm, he lifted one side off the floor and tilted the table over on to Rory's knees. As Rory stepped back the injured man leapt towards him and swung a crashing left-hand blow to his head. He followed up by throwing his whole body at him, causing Rory to drop his handgun.

They fell to the ground together and Rory hit his head on the wall as he went. Half-stunned, Rory struggled with the man on top of him, who had now got his left hand to Rory's throat.

Rory managed to grab the injured right arm,

however. He twisted it and heard the already-damaged bones break like a giant nut being cracked open. The pain must have been excruciating, for his opponent relaxed his grip sufficiently for Rory to struggle from under him on to his knees and land a full-blooded punch straight to the man's jaw. As his opponent's head sagged, Rory quickly landed two more punches with a strength he didn't know he possessed. He was relieved to see the stranger falling to the dusty wooden floor, offering no further resistance. As he tried to clear his own fuzzy head, Rory heard Marshal Mason's distinctive voice.

'Well done, young Tex. I reckon I owe you a pretty big debt of gratitude. Those two were sure determined to put an end to me, and I think they would have got away with it if you hadn't showed up.'

As he spoke, the marshal grabbed the collar of the man Rory had knocked out, and effortlessly dragged him towards the cell, where he had already ensconced his companion.

'I suppose we better get the doc to that one you shot. He's gonna be suffering when he comes round, but I reckon you and me deserve a celebratory drop of whiskey before we worry about him. Sit yourself down, young Tex, while I dig a bottle out of this overturned table.'

'Marshal, I got something to tell you,' Rory blurted out as the lawman poured drinks into a couple of none-too-clean glasses he had brought through from his bunkroom. 'My real name ain't

Tex Wilson. I used it because I think I'm being followed.'

'Better tell me about it,' said the marshal.

He then listened patiently while Rory related the
whole story, including the admission that he had
knifed his uncle, David Pritchard. 'And my real name
is Rory Rimmer,' he ended his tale.

Suddenly, the marshal jerked up from the
slumped position he had taken whilst listening to
Rory's story. There was incredulity in his squeaky
voice. 'Rimmer, did you say? That's a pretty uncom-
mon name. What was your pa's first name and where
do you come from?'

'His name was Jack, and we come from an area
called Peterland Valley. Why?'

Marshal Mason looked stunned. It took him a
couple of minutes to respond. 'Jack Rimmer. Jack
Rimmer. Well, I'll be damned, boy. I thought there
was something familiar about you with that crop of
fair curly hair you had when you first arrived in town,
but then you had it cut and I didn't give it no more
thought.'

The marshal rose from his chair, came round the
desk and placed a hand on Rory's shoulder. 'Ain't
that the strangest thing,' he said. 'Jack Rimmer was
the closest buddy I ever had. We rode out together
over twenty years ago. We was gonna see the world
together, but we only made it to that valley of yours.
He fell in a big way for this cute little thing with blue
eyes and a smile as big as the Rio Grande. I confess I
tried to get him to continue with me but I couldn't

drag him away and eventually had to ride out alone. So you're Jack Rimmer's son. My buddy's son. I can hardly believe it.'

There was a combination of sadness and anger in the marshal's voice as he repeated the central part of Rory's story. 'And he died on the end of a rope!' As he spoke, he poured them both another whiskey and proceeded to tell Rory about his relationship with his father some twenty years earlier.

'I never had a friend like your pa,' he said. 'Not before or since. Saddest day in my whole life when he said he had changed his mind about us riding the world together. Funny what a gal can do to a man. Your ma had a hold on him like a powerful magnet. Right from the start, though, it was clear there was gonna be trouble with those brothers of hers.'

'What do you mean?' asked Rory.

'Well, they were very possessive – regarded your ma as some kind of fragile doll. They couldn't understand it when she took your father back to their ranch and said she was gonna marry him. Jack and me was just intending to rest a few days in that pretty valley of yours, but he met her in the store where she helped out with the orderin' and keepin' the accounts. I had to go huntin' for Jack and found that the two of them had been sittin' and talkin' for nearly four hours non-stop.

'The very next day Jack asked her to marry him and ride out with us. I told him it was crazy but he was dead set on it. Trouble was that she agreed to marry him but said she wasn't gonna leave Peterland, so Jack just said that was it. He would have to stay, too.

'Her brothers told your mother she was insane, mixing with a stranger like him, and tried to scare him off. Told him to leave, or else. But when that didn't work, they changed tactics and offered him money to leave. They all had a flaming row, with Jack accusing them of being Southern bigots. In the end, there was nothin' the brothers could do to dissuade either of them from plannin' to go ahead with the marriage, but it was pretty plain they was never gonna approve of your father. Him bein' a Catholic didn't help.'

Rory cut into the marshal's narrative. 'I didn't know that,' he said. 'He never told me.'

'No,' continued the marshal, 'he wouldn't have, because he promised your mother he'd drop his religion so they could get married. But the brothers, especially the eldest one, David, would never accept it. He told your pa that, if he ever let your ma down, he'd kill him. Sounds like he did, too, even though it took him half a lifetime to carry out his threat.'

Marshal Mason paused for a while, gulped down the last of his whiskey and finished his story. 'I didn't stay for the wedding, even though Jack begged me to. I guess I was angry at the way things had turned out. I rode out alone, and never heard of him since. Least not until you turned up in Bush Creek, young fella.'

Abraham Mason took another slug of whiskey. 'So your father did eventually ride out, but only after your mother died. She was sure some special woman to hold him like that.'

'Sure was,' said Rory, with tears in his eyes.

CHAPTER
TWENTY-ONE

Rory was absorbed in the task he was undertaking: painting a new sign for the Lucky Horseshoe saloon. It was not work he had attempted before and it was taking all his concentration, when suddenly from behind him came a terrified scream from Julie. But her yell was choked off as the stranger tightened the grip his left arm had around her throat, whilst the pistol in his right was pointed into her side.

Rory reeled round in alarm, knocking the paint over his carefully executed artwork as he did so.

Immediately he recognized the man who had Julie in his grip. He was no stranger. It was his mother's brother, Frank Pritchard.

And alongside him, his rifle pointed at Rory, was the other brother, Jake.

'We guessed it might be you,' growled Frank. 'We been huntin' you a long while and heard about a young fella who had ridden in here about the time we started out lookin' for you.'

Rory stayed frozen. With horror, he realized that, stupidly, he had unbuckled his belt and left his gun on the veranda, about six feet away, while he had concentrated on the sign-painting.

As he looked across at it Frank warned: 'Don't even think about it, or the girl is finished. Fella on the trail told us about how the stranger had gone sweet on a girl and how the law had gone soft too and let him free after killin' and horsethieving. Well, we ain't goin' soft. You're gonna pay for what you done to David.'

As he spoke, Julie's father, reacting to her scream, came rushing round the corner of the building with an ancient shotgun in his scrawny hands. As he took in the scene, he instinctively levelled the weapon and was immediately gunned down by Frank. Julie's father took Pritchard's bullet full in the chest, but as he fell he also managed to fire.

Jake Pritchard looked down in disbelief as the blood oozed out of the multiple wounds peppering his body. He half-turned towards his brother, as if seeking help, before slowly sliding to the dusty ground, face down, with his blood spreading out from under him. As he let out a deep groan that signalled the end of his life, his brother Frank relaxed his grip on Julie.

She squirmed away from him at the same time as Rory dived towards his own gun on the veranda. He was too slow though. He had only just got his hand on the holstered weapon when Frank Pritchard snarled: 'Hold it, Rory Rimmer, or you're a dead man.'

Rory looked up and understood that he was at a severe disadvantage. Having lost his hold on Julie, Pritchard now had his Colt pointed at his nephew.

'Leave the gun and stand up,' he ordered. 'Otherwise I'll kill the both of you here and now.'

Rory considered his position, and accepted that he had no choice, especially when Pritchard called out: 'Come here, Ned.'

From the corner of the next building the lanky ranch-hand Ned limped across with a rifle at the ready.

'Cover them,' ordered Pritchard, as he moved to check on his brother, carefully turning the body over before quickly coming to the obvious conclusion. 'He's dead because of you, Rory Rimmer. Damn you. You're sure gonna pay.'

For a moment it looked as if he was indeed going to kill Rory out of his cold anger, but he controlled himself and instead walked over so that he could kick Rory's revolver way out of reach.

He then took the Winchester from Ned and ordered the ranch-hand to fetch their horses. Ned had walked about twenty paces when a shrill voice called out.

'Now, you fellas, just stay where you are.' The whine was unmistakable. It came from above, where Marshal Mason was standing on an upper-level balcony of the Lucky Horseshoe.

Pritchard looked up in surprise. He hesitated but,

deciding to ignore the marshal's order, raised the rifle and fired upwards.

An angry shriek of pain came from above, indicating that the marshal had been hit, but he again shouted a warning. 'I said stay where you are.'

Alarmed that the marshal was still alive, Pritchard once more decided to ignore the warning. He quickly fired a random shot up to the balcony and then shot at Rory as he started to run in the direction already taken by Ned. But in his haste he missed his target and his bullet dug into the ground by Rory's feet.

Watching the scene, Ned decided that a hasty departure was also his best course of action. He fired off a wild shot as he took off, sprinting as fast as his damaged leg would carry him to the shelter of the nearest building.

Marshal Mason fired after him, but missed. He shouted down to Rory: 'Go get them, son. I've been shot in the leg.'

With a quick glance at Julie, Rory did as he had been told. He stooped to pick up the rifle Jake Pritchard had dropped and raced after Ned. As he turned the corner where the ranch-hand had gone, he was greeted by another shot, which thudded into the building's woodwork beside him.

Rory ducked back round the corner and decided that his best bet was to skirt right round the building rather than expose himself again. When he had done so he peered round the corner and could see Ned crouched down behind some stacked logs, still

looking in the opposite direction, where he expected
the pursuit to come from.

Rory's first instinct was simply to shoot from where
he was and carry on after Frank Pritchard. He had a
good view of Ned's side and thought he had a rea-
sonable chance of hitting him. He wanted to make
sure, though, so he decided that he would go round
one more building, so that he could approach from
behind.

As he did so, he came face to face with John
Gibson, the man who had threatened Mrs Penney.
He had evidently heard the firing and was moving
down the alley between the two buildings towards the
area where the shooting had taken place.

Gibson was the first to react. Instantly recognizing
Rory, he lunged out at him and successfully landed a
mighty blow to his chest, which pushed Rory back
against the building. Quickly Gibson followed up
with two more blows and Rory felt his head swimming. Instinctively, though, he hit back and – more
by luck than careful aiming – landed a solid blow on
Gibson's chin. His dazed opponent stepped backwards and Rory managed to get in two more hefty
blows. Though somewhat surprised by his own
success, he was delighted to see Gibson sink to the
ground. Rory picked up a length of wood leaning
against the building and unceremoniously cracked
Gibson over the head with it.

As Gibson lay still – clearly unconscious – Rory
retrieved the rifle and continued towards where the
ranch-hand Ned had been. This took him three or

four minutes to achieve, and when he had completed his manoeuvre he saw Ned peering over his makeshift defensive barricade, but beginning to edge backwards.

Rory completed his encircling and was standing not twenty yards behind Ned, who now ducked down behind an old wagon, still looking in the opposite direction to where Rory stood. Rory advanced cautiously, with any sound he might have made disguised by the cackling of some hens.

Eventually he stood immediately behind the ranch-hand. He was again sorely tempted simply to shoot the man who, after all, was one of his father's two murderers.

Resisting the temptation, he touched the tip of the rifle barrel between the man's shoulder blades. 'I'll sure delight in shootin' you dead if you don't drop your weapons immediately,' he said.

Without argument Ned did so, and was actually quite relieved to see an injured marshal come round the corner towards them, followed by Julie.

The marshal hobbled over. 'I don't take kindly to people shootin' at me,' he whined at Ned. Together the marshal and Rory – with one arm round Julie – took Ned to jail, collecting a recovering John Gibson on the way.

'What happened to the other one?' asked the marshal.

'I heard him ride off when I was sneaking up on this one,' Rory replied as he pointed at Ned Pointing. 'I reckon you guessed, Marshal, that these were the men I told you about. The one shot by Julie's pa was one of my uncles, Jake, and the one who escaped is Frank. This one here is the ranch-hand Ned who was at the hangin' with their elder brother, David.'

CHAPTER TWENTY-TWO

Judge Jennings was none too pleased to be called back to Bush Creek so soon, this time for a double trial.

For a little town they seemed to be having a lot of trouble. He was particularly vexed to hear that one of the defendants was again to be Tex Wilson – though he was now called Rory Rimmer, having voluntarily revealed his true identity to the town's marshal and admitted to stabbing a man to death some weeks earlier, apparently before the events he had already been tried for.

In a counter claim, another man now being held by the marshal was accused by Rimmer of illegally hanging his father. All very confusing. Once there, though, the judge soon sorted it out with quickly arranged trials.

Ned Pointing talked eagerly in an attempt to save his own skin, especially anxious to make it clear that he had only taken part in the hanging of Jack Rimmer because his boss had ordered him to. He said he had been a ranch-hand with the Pritchards for eight years and confirmed that there had been a long-standing feud between Rory's father and the three brothers, with David Pritchard particularly antagonistic towards his brother-in-law. He told how he had once heard David accuse Jack Rimmer of being an opportunist who had married his sister just in the hope of getting a share in the ranch.

Judge Jennings dismissed this as inadmissible hearsay evidence but the jury were extremely attentive when Ned Pointing was asked to describe what had happened after Jack Rimmer and his son Rory had left the ranch, following the death of Ann.

'I heard a terrible row that night,' testified Pointing. 'David tried to persuade his brothers that they should follow Jack and Rory and bring them back to justice. He blamed Jack for his sister's death, even though she had told the doctor and the sheriff that her injured head had been caused by an accidental fall.'

When questioned, Pointing told how – on David Pritchard's insistence – Ann had been examined by the town's doctor, who had pronounced that the bruises were consistent with a fall but they were superficial and there should be no lasting damage.

'He was wrong, of course,' Pointing added, 'because her death was obviously caused by the head injury. But no action was taken because she had already sworn that it was all an accident.'

Pointing continued his testimony by talking more about the argument between the Pritchard brothers. He said he had overheard David shouting that Jack Rimmer had to pay for killing Ann.

'The other two brothers said to let matters be, but David insisted he was going to track down the father and son, and drag them back. He ordered that I ride with him the next day,' continued Pointing. 'When we caught up with them he started ranting at Jack Rimmer. They fought, then David said he was gonna string him up for killing his sister, since the law was clearly not gonna do anything about it.'

'I told him I wanted nothin' to do with a hangin', but he said if I didn't do as I was told I could expect a bullet to the head myself. He was like a madman. I was real scared,' continued Ned. 'I had no choice but to go along with what he was determined to do.'

In his evidence, Rory Rimmer confirmed that this had indeed appeared to be the case, with Ned Pointing being an unwilling accomplice rather than a prime mover, though he still recalled with horror the way Ned had casually swung his father's suspended body to check whether he was dead.

Ned also confirmed that David Pritchard had kicked the boy whilst he was on the ground and threatened him with being shot so that he couldn't report the hanging.

'So the boy had just been forced to watch his father's hanging and then had his own life threatened?' the judge asked.

'Yes, that's right,' agreed Ned.

'So you could say he was fearful for his own life and killed Pritchard in self-defence?'

'Yes . . . but no,' replied Ned.

The judge bristled. 'What the hell do you mean? How can it be yes *and* no?'

Ned, looking really rattled, stammered his answer. 'Well, your honour, you asked two questions. It was true that the boy was threatened, and it's certainly true that he stabbed my boss. But he didn't kill him.'

At this the court erupted, and Judge Jennings had considerable difficulty getting the silence he demanded.

'What do you mean? The boy has already admitted he killed his uncle.'

'No, no. He didn't die. His wounds were bad but I managed to patch him up and get him back to the nearest town for the doc to see to him. He reckoned the boss will probably never get back the proper use of his legs but he's still alive. It was the boss who told me to go back to the ranch and get his brothers to track down young Rory.'

In the now stunned court-room, Pointing rushed ahead with his story. 'The boss said I wasn't to tell the sheriff, because if the law caught up with the boy before we did, then he would tell about the hangin' and we could both finish up with ropes around our necks. So I did what he said. I went back for Frank and Jake, and we all went back to bury Jack and start our search for his son. That's how we got to be here.'

The court again broke out into a noisy hubbub but the judge was determined to close the case against

Ned Pointing, whose involvement in the illegal hanging was now beyond dispute. To tidy things up, though, he called for evidence from Marshal Mason, who explained how the two remaining Pritchard brothers and Pointing had come to Bush Creek and were threatening to kill Rory and the girl. He described the shooting, and praised Rory's action in capturing Ned Pointing.

Commenting that all the pieces of evidence seemed to add up and reinforce each other, Judge Jennings included a personal aside in his summing up. 'All this could have been avoided. I still don't understand why, if he was so unhappy for so many years, Jack Rimmer just didn't ride off earlier and leave the brothers and his wife behind. Quitting on a woman ain't no crime,' he mused. 'They say Sam Houston did it twice.' He smiled, then added: 'Hell, I even did it myself.'

With that, he accepted the jury's unhesitating guilty verdict against Ned Pointing and sentenced him to five years in jail for complicity in a hanging. Without wasting time on a separate trial, he immediately went on to rule that Rory Rimmer had no case to answer, since the stabbing was clearly in self-defence.

Cleared of all charges, Rory was a free man. But so, still, were his father's murderer, David Pritchard, and Frank Pritchard, who had killed Julie's pea.

CHAPTER TWENTY-THREE

'Well, son, I reckon it will be a coupla weeks before I'll be fit enough to chase after those uncles of yours. Meanwhile, we'll bury young Julie's pa in a fittin' manner. If he hadn't showed up and killed that Jake I guess things might have turned out a little differently. But first, let's get you made my deputy so that you can come with me on an official basis.'

Rory was rather taken by surprise, since he hadn't really been thinking ahead to what would happen next. He turned to Julie.

'What do you think? I don't want to leave you, but should I go?'

'Of course you should. I want Pa's killer caught and you must want justice for your father's hangin'. We can't let them get away with it, can we?'

Having gained Julie's support, Rory turned to practical matters.

'How we gonna find them?' he asked the marshal.

'Surely we won't be able to track Frank on such a cold trail.'

'Don't you worry about that, young Rory. It's not just a question of following hoof-prints you know. I've tracked down men who've had a far longer start than Frank. The important part is figurin' out where they are going to head. Frank won't just wander off into the blue horizon. There's basically two things he'll want to do. One is get back home to the ranch, and the other is to link up with his injured brother, David – the one you knifed.'

Rory was excited and yet fearful at the idea that he was to accompany the marshal in a search for Frank and David Pritchard. He had felt tremendous relief when he heard Ned Pointing's court-room evidence that his uncle David was still alive, and that his stabbing – though serious – had not been fatal. Ever since the day of his father's hanging, Rory had carried with him an abhorrence of what David Pritchard had done but combined this emotion with the disconcerting thought that he himself was also a killer. He had tried to assuage his feelings of guilt by convincing himself that he had really been given no choice. His own life had been threatened and he had acted in self-defence.

Despite this knowledge, however, he had not been able to persuade himself that the concept of an eye for an eye was justified. Having been convinced in his own mind that he was guilty of murder, Rory's conscience had remained troubled and his feelings of

138

guilt were compounded by the fact that he had acted like a guilty man by fleeing the scene, then adopting an alias, and in not revealing his actions to the proper law authorities.

Now, however, Rory was relieved to find that he could focus on the idea that it was the two remaining Pritchard brothers who were on the wrong side of the law, and the marshal was giving him a chance to act within the law and bring them to justice. Somewhat to his surprise, he actually found himself becoming impatient to get on their trail.

Meanwhile, as they waited for Marshal Mason's injury to heal, he continued to occupy himself by undertaking some of the jobs around town that had previously been Paul Denham's responsibility but had been considerably neglected over recent months or even postponed for years.

The widow, Mrs Penney, had moved into town and the new owner of her homestead, Mr Pollock, had continued to employ Rory to get the place up and running properly after the lack of attention it had suffered during Mr Penney's illness. Whilst the two men undertook the more demanding tasks, Mrs Penney and Julie also spent some time undertaking less physical activities such as feeding the hens and fitting new curtains.

Mr Pollock was delighted with their combined efforts and was effusive in his thanks. He then took the whole of the town by surprise when he announced that he was soon to be joined by a young lady from the East who, after correspondence over the past couple of months, had agreed to come and be his bride. Knowing the considerable shortage of eligible females in the area, the people of Bush Creek had assumed that thirty-seven-year-old Walter Pollock was destined to remain a bachelor, and they were delighted to hear his news.

There was one exception, however. John Gibson still held a grudge against Mrs Penney for selling her property to Mr Pollock rather than him, and an even bigger grudge against Rory Rimmer after their two previous run-ins had both gone in the younger man's favour.

Early one morning Gibson again showed up at the homestead, still with a determination to obtain the property. His first effort was to try to persuade Mr Pollock to sign over the homestead for the same price he had paid Mrs Penney. When this offer was turned down, Gibson offered to pay a little more, but Mr Pollock continued to rebuff him, explaining that he was to be married and that he could not risk disappointing his future bride by not offering her the life he had promised in his letters.

Suddenly, Gibson lost his temper. 'I promise you she'll face a life that will be nothing like you've promised,' he shouted. 'I'll make you a promise, Pollock. As soon as you get her back here from the church, I'll be round to visit your new bride, and I doubt that she'll much like my attentions. And every time you leave her alone out here, or even turn your back, I'll be here. You'll never be able to feel she's safe. Your life, and hers, will be hell. That's my promise to you, old man.'

'You bastard, Gibson. You can't frighten me into—'

Pollock's protestations were silenced by a vicious blow to the head from the bigger man.

When Rory and Julie arrived at the homestead a little later they found Mr Pollock suffering from his physical defeat, but still mentally strong enough not to want Gibson to get his way. Angry and bitter, he told them that, after the beating, he had been forced to sign a paper agreeing that he would sell the property to Gibson.

Enraged at what had happened, Rory was all set to chase after Gibson, but was persuaded by Julie to cool down and report to Marshal Mason while she stayed with Mr Pollock. Although clearly badly bruised, he appeared to have no broken bones or other serious injuries and insisted that Rory should ride into town right away.

'I never liked that Gibson,' the marshal spat out when Rory reported to him. 'Pity we couldn't hold him longer for delaying you when you was chasing those fellas after the shootin'. But I'll tell you that the coupla days I had him locked up were enough to persuade me he was a nasty piece of work. So let's go pull him in. I reckon my leg is OK for me just to ride out to his place. It ain't that far.'

When they got there the marshal insisted on taking no chances. He waited hidden out the front of Gibson's place, while Rory worked his way around the back. It was something of a ramshackle place that

Gibson lived in alone, and it somewhat belied the amount of money he was rumoured to have gained from a wife he had married in Fort Worth but who had lasted only a few months when he had brought her back to Bush Creek. The other women in town said she was like a fish out of water, and no one was surprised when – without a word to anyone – she simply disappeared. Gibson just said that she had gone back where she had come from and it was 'good riddance' as far as he was concerned.

She hadn't been much liked, and the citizens of Bush Creek were prepared to agree with her husband's assessment of the situation, even though there were a few wild rumours that he had possibly done away with her and that she was buried somewhere.

Rory made a wide circuit of the building and crept round the side when he heard the marshal call for Gibson to reveal himself. There was silence, and the marshal called out again. 'Come out of there, Gibson, and give yourself up.'

His reply was a shot from a window in the front of the building, and Rory could see the marshal retreat to make sure he was out of Gibson's range. Guessing that Gibson had no intention of surrendering or even exposing himself to a return of fire, Rory retraced his steps round to the back of the building, where he knew there was another doorway. To his surprise, he found it was unbolted so he silently let himself inside and crept forward to where he could peer round and see Gibson's back.

'Drop your gun, and freeze,' Rory ordered, at the same time as the marshal fired at the house and hit a bell hanging over the front porch. Rory's command, the marshal's shot and the ringing of the bell all combined to confuse Gibson, but he spun round and loosed off a hurried shot in Rory's direction. The bullet logged itself harmlessly in the wooden partition wall and Rory ducked back round the doorframe, as Gibson fired again without having a target to aim at.

Hearing movement, Rory retreated and slid back through the door he had used to enter the building. There was again silence, but then Rory heard Gibson coming forward again so he moved back further round to position himself behind a water butt. Whilst he waited for Gibson's next move he heard another shot from the marshal at the front of the building.

Suddenly Gibson rushed out of the back door a few feet from where Rory was crouched. But, fortunately, he looked in the wrong direction and in those few seconds Rory carefully shot at his opponent's leg. Gibson crumpled to the ground and winded himself but still managed to hang on to his Colt. Not wishing to shoot again, Rory charged forward and kicked the weapon out of Gibson's grasp. But Gibson grabbed his foot as he did so, and pulled Rory down on top of him.

For a second time, Rory found himself in Gibson's strong bear hug with his arms pinned to his side. He struggled to free himself but could only manage to twist to the side, without freeing himself from

143

Gibson's grasp. Unexpectedly, though, the pressure was released and his assailant went limp.

Rory looked up, and saw the marshal standing over them with his rifle butt facing down over Gibson's head.

'Reckon he might have a bit of a bump tomorrow.' The marshal smiled. 'But he sure asked for it, resisting arrest like that, and shootin' at a lawman.' As he spoke, he used his foot to turn Gibson's body over but winced with pain as he did so.

'You OK, Marshal?'

'Yep, but I reckon I shouldn't have tried to run on this gammy leg. Heard the shots, though, and thought you might be in trouble, so I had no choice. Perhaps it's a good job I got here when I did, though I reckon you handled yourself pretty well, young fella. Looks like you're gonna make a good deputy. Now, before you get yourself up off the ground, see what Gibson's got tucked inside his shirt.'

Rory leant over, pulled out a few sheets of paper and examined them. 'Looks like the document he got Mr Pollock to sign, Marshal.'

'Reckon so. Now there's two ways we can handle this. The official way is to keep these papers as evidence and face the possibility that Gibson might get a clever lawyer man and somehow make these documents stand up in court so that Pollock and his bride lose their homestead.' He paused. 'The other way is that these papers simply disappear. Which way do you favour, young fella?'

Rory looked up and smiled at the marshal. 'Think

I'd better find a match and have a little fire.'

'There now. I said you've got the makings of a good lawman who knows what's really right or wrong.'

CHAPTER TWENTY-FOUR

In fact, it was nearly a month after what the Bush Creek community now called 'The shoot-out day' before the marshal was ready to ride out after the two remaining Pritchard brothers, and he decided that, even though it would be slower, he would take a light-weight wagon to ease the strain on his leg wound.

Using the not-too-subtle technique of withholding food from his prisoner, he had little trouble getting the ranch-hand Ned to reveal that, after the hanging, he had returned first to Peterland Valley and had then taken Frank and Jake back to where Jack Rimmer's body had been left suspended on a rope. They had cut him down and buried him in a shallow ravine a few hundred yards away, before going to the small town where Ned had earlier taken the injured David in order to recover. Then they had continued the search that eventually led them to Bush Creek.

Now Frank and David were the ones to be hunted.

Marshal Mason decided that the scene of the hanging was where he and Rory should start. Following Ned Pointing's instructions, they found the spot with no real difficulty and discovered the body hidden in a dip and covered in rocks. It was a grisly business recovering the remains, and Rory forced himself to somehow make a distinction between this rotting corpse and the man who had nurtured him for nineteen years.

Marshal Mason, whilst silently acknowledging the suffering Rory must be feeling as they uncovered the body, stayed stony-faced as they placed the remains into a casket brought from Bush Creek in the wagon. His face was set in an expression that was as hard as the rocks which had covered his buddy's remains. The only words he spoke were addressed to Rory in a determined voice as he closed the coffin lid.

'Rest assured, son, we'll give him a decent burial alongside your ma when we get to Peterland Valley, and then we are goin' to get those brothers. I promise you.'

When they arrived at Peterland the marshal instructed Rory to stay in an empty line shack just outside the town, as he didn't want anyone to recognize him at this stage.

Rory protested that he wanted to go back to the ranch to confront his relatives, but eventually accepted the marshal's advice when he explained that he wanted to go alone to see the county sheriff to find out what he knew about the family feud.

147

At first Sheriff Warner had been reluctant to accept the marshal's story of the recent events.

'But the Pritchards are a well-respected family around these parts,' he asserted. 'They wouldn't be involved in anything like a hangin' or a shoot-out.' He had no alternative explanation, however, for why all three brothers hadn't been seen around lately and had to accept that the body in the coffin was pretty damning evidence that there had been some kind of foul play. When pressed, he acknowledged that he had heard rumours about a Pritchard family row after the death of Ann Rimmer.

When Marshal Mason produced an arrest warrant for Frank Pritchard, the sheriff reluctantly committed himself to riding out to the Pritchards' ranch, but he resisted Abraham Mason's suggestion that he should go, too. 'You stay and make the arrangements for Rimmer's funeral,' he insisted. 'I'll investigate out at the ranch.'

When he arrived back in the town, the sheriff reported that he had questioned the wives at the ranch. They had confirmed that Frank had indeed returned there alone, but they claimed that – despite their protestations – he had again ridden out, saying he was going to search for his two missing brothers. He had told the wives he suspected that their menfolk might be in some kind of trouble with the Rimmer couple, Jack and his son Rory.

The sheriff went on to indicate that he intended to take no further action, unless any of the brothers returned to town, and that he didn't want to investigate the alleged hanging of Jack Rimmer, as his death had clearly occurred outside his area of jurisdiction.

Jack Rimmer's burial was an entirely private affair, with only Marshal Mason and Rory in attendance. Rory had been insistent that he did not want to tell the Pritchard family, and the marshal cautioned him against contacting any friends or acquaintances his father might have had. 'Remember,' he said, 'that you and your pa had your chance to say farewell before the two of you rode out of Peterland. Best left at that, I think, especially since it's not a good idea for the family to hear that you have returned, though it is possible that the sheriff has already told them. Despite his badge, I'm not entirely sure I trust that fella. Seems to me he might be more interested in stayin' well in with the Pritchard family and their neighbours than he is in gettin' at the truth. I reckon it's gonna be up to you and me to get to the end of this business.'

'OK. But where we gonna start? How we gonna find Frank – or David?'

'Well, first off we'll go out to the ranch ourselves . . . but we're not gonna' get there until dusk.'

When they arrived, they tied the horses some distance away, and then placed themselves in some bushes that gave them a good view of the ranch house and the adjoining barns. They had waited less than an hour before the marshal's intuition proved to be spot on, when a woman came out of the house carrying a basket.

'That's Frank's wife, Betty,' said Rory.

'Guessed right, then, didn't I? The sheriff obviously told them I was here asking questions, and that gave them a warning. I'll wager a month's pay that Frank is hiding out in that barn she's goin' in to.'

When Betty came out nearly an hour later, the marshal chuckled. 'Well, I reckon Frank's had his oats. We'll give him a while and then go inside.'

As they quietly entered the barn, the marshal chuckled again. 'Listen to that snoring,' he whispered. 'Ain't exactly difficult to know where he is when he makes a noise like that. Let's spoil his dreams.'

When the marshal's Colt was jabbed at Frank's throat it acted as a pretty effective wake-up signal. Frank offered no resistance when he was frog-marched to the wagon which had been used to transport Jack Rimmer's coffin.

'Bet his wife is puzzled in the mornin'. She feeds him, gives him a bit of loving, and the next thing she knows is that he has disappeared. Her husband has gone, but no horse is missing. She'll have trouble working that one out.'

When they were on the trail away from Peterland, the marshal did not have much difficulty getting Frank Pritchard to direct them to the small township where Ned Pointing had taken the badly injured brother, David, after the hanging.

Now, with a gun in his back, Frank led Marshal Mason and Rory up the stairs of the lodging house where David was recuperating. The woman running the place had recognized Frank from his earlier visit and did not demur when he said he had brought a couple of buddies to visit his brother. The marshal nudged Frank through the door into the room where David was in bed, and had a feeling of deep satisfaction when, for the first time, he came face to face with the man who had strung up his one-time buddy.

'David Pritchard,' he said in a calm voice that betrayed his inner anger, 'I'm arresting you for the murder of Jack Rimmer. You're coming to Bush Creek to stand trial.'

Pritchard's face showed his fear. He turned to his brother. 'Frank, for pity's sake, do something.'

The marshal's voice somehow lost its usual shrill tone as he snarled at both brothers. 'He ain't gonna be doin' nothin' that will help you. He's gonna stand trial himself for killing an old man in my town, and he's gonna pay – just like you. Rory, you get Frank downstairs. Make sure you keep him covered. We don't want no clever tricks. I'll look after this one.'

CHAPTER
TWENTY-FIVE

Rory Rimmer was never sure exactly what happened in that bedroom after he had taken Frank Pritchard down the stairs. He never dared to question the marshal about it, but retained an unvoiced suspicion that events had not been quite as the lawman later told the judge and county sheriff back in Bush Creek.

Abraham Mason's story was that he had started to get David Pritchard out of the bed, but the injured man had grabbed at a revolver sitting on a window ledge and the marshal had been forced to defend himself. Rory had heard no sign of a struggle, however, and had been surprised when the marshal had appeared downstairs with a body over his shoulder. David's dead body . . . with clear strangulation marks round the neck.

Judge Jennings did not attempt to disguise his dismay at once again being called back to Bush

152

Creek. 'Damnation,' he complained. 'I seem to spend more time in this lousy hick town than I do anywhere else in the Territory. Wouldn't mind if you had a half-decent hotel, but it seems to me that you get so few people through here that the dust lies thicker indoors than it does outside. So what is it this time?' he asked the unctuous leader of the town council, who revelled in the title of mayor.

Carefully disregarding the judge's unflattering comments about his town, the aptly-named Charles Precious summarized the reason for the recall of his visitor. 'My goodness, your honour, you'll hardly credit what we've been through. First there was the marshal being attacked in his own office by two ruffians he had dealt with in the past. Then, as you know, some other fellows arrived and there was a mighty shoot-out, with old man Denham and one of the gunmen being killed. Then the marshal takes off with the young fella you tried before. Then the two of them come back with a prisoner and a dead man in a wagon.' Sweating profusely, and constantly twisting his hands together in his excitable state, the town's official representative could hardly contain himself as he gabbled out the series of remarkable events that had taken place.

'Calm down, man,' the judge ordered. 'Seems to me this place is getting out of hand. Perhaps I had better get a US marshal in before things get totally out of control.'

'No, no, sir. I assure you there's no need for that. Our own lawman has done a remarkable job, I assure you. We're all right behind him, and I really don't think there'll be more trouble once you've hung the guy who killed old man Denham.'

The judge bristled at this effrontery. 'I'll remind you,' he barked, 'that there has to be a fair trial before there's any talk of a hanging.'

Realizing that he had unwittingly overstepped the mark, Precious quickly backed down with profuse apologies and a conciliatory offer to escort the judge to the saloon for a drop or two of whiskey. Remembering that, against all his initial expectations, the Lucky Horseshoe stocked a particularly fine Kentucky bourbon, the judge was not slow to accept the hospitality offered and ensconce himself in the bar which would, once more, serve as his court-room.

Once again, however, the trial was to be a relatively fast process. The judge had already passed his judgment on Ned Pointing and was quite ready to accept Rory Rimmer's evidence that the body Marshal Mason had now brought back to Bush Creek was indeed that of David Pritchard, the prime mover in the illegal hanging of Rory's father. Since he was dead, the man could hardly give evidence in his own defence and even his accomplice, Ned Pointing, had corroborated Rory Rimmer's oath that this was the man who had strung up his father. Eager to get through the business as quickly as possible, the judge was happy to cast aside the fact that David Pritchard's body had carried the signs of previous knife wounds and he didn't bother to question Marshal Mason's testimony that he had been forced to strangle Pritchard in self-defence whilst trying to arrest him.

The judge's main concern was with the trial of the man the marshal had brought in alive, Frank Pritchard.

The accused man's lawyer used the only defence line open to him, by arguing the case that Frank had really been acting in self-defence when he shot Julie's father, Paul Denham. He argued that old man Denham had rushed round the corner in a frenzy and was likely to kill anyone he thought was threatening his daughter. But Pritchard was unable to answer satisfactorily the challenging questions as to why the two brothers had come to Bush Creek in the first place and why they had been holding Rory and Julie at gunpoint if they meant them no physical harm.

'We just wanted to make sure Rory Rimmer stood trial for knifing my brother,' Pritchard protested. 'We was gonna hand him over to the law.'

But his protestations carried little weight when it came to the details of the actual shooting. Julie, Rory and – most important – Marshal Mason, all testified that it was Frank who had fired first, and that Paul Denham had only killed Jake as he fell to the ground with Frank Pritchard's bullet already in his body. They all pointed out that Frank had been holding Julie captive, so there was no way that her father would have fired his shotgun at Frank.

The argument of self-defence was firmly ruled out

by the judge, who virtually ordered the jury to bring in a verdict of murder. Frank Pritchard was to be consigned to the county jail and would end his life dangling on the end of a rope.

Three months later, Rory, Julie and Marshal Mason stood beside the twin graves of Ann and Jack Rimmer in Peterland Valley's cemetery.

In the period since Frank Pritchard's lawful hanging for murdering Julie's father, old Paul Denham, she had discovered that the loss of her virginity in the Metzner household had also been the start of her pregnancy. When the doctor confirmed the news, Rory and Julie had hastily arranged to be married.

They had intended it to be a low-key affair but news had soon spread and nearly all the townsfolk, and many from the surrounding countryside, made it their business to attend the church. The couple were now big news in Bush Creek and few people wanted to miss out on the wedding of their deputy marshal and his young bride.

Soon after the wedding, the marshal had returned with the newly-weds to Peterland Valley. His first action was to visit the county sheriff, who was sitting behind his desk smoking a cheroot.

'You lied to me,' said the marshal, leaning over the desk and jabbing a finger at Sheriff Warner.

'What?'

'You told me you went to the Pritchards' ranch and that there was no sign of Frank Pritchard.'

156

'That's right. His wife Betty told me he'd come back but then left again the followin' day to find his brothers.'

'Not true, Sheriff. I found him there that same night and arrested him. You knew I was huntin' him for murder in my town, so you should have brought him to me.'

The sheriff stubbed out his cheroot and rose from his chair to face his accuser.

'I told you before that he was not there.'

'Don't think you looked very hard, 'cause I found him in a barn that same night. I'm bettin' you knew he was there and were covering up for him.'

'That, Marshal, is a serious charge and one you can't prove.'

'But that's where you're wrong, Warner. I can prove it. While he was in my custody, Frank Pritchard signed a statement to say that he spoke to you that day and you said you would cover for him in return for a promise of cash. In my book that makes you a pretty corrupt lawman.'

The sheriff visibly paled and sank back into his chair. 'What you gonna do about it?' he asked.

'Well, this might surprise you, but I've thought it over and I ain't gonna do anything – for now, at least. Pritchard might be dead but I'm keepin' that piece of paper,' said the marshal, delighted that his guess had been correct but keeping a poker-straight face as he lied about the non-existent evidence. 'But you ought to know,' he continued, 'that young Rory Rimmer is plannin' on coming back to Peterland

Valley to settle here with his new wife and I expect you, Sheriff Warner, to make sure he gets any help or support he needs. I'll be keeping in touch so make sure I never have to produce Pritchard's statement.'

With that, Marshal Mason left the shaken sheriff and then made sure that the local newspaper editor got the juicy story that the Pritchard brothers were now all dead and that their nephew Rory had been cleared of all charges previously made against him and was back to lay claim to his share of the family ranch.

To Rory's surprise, the Pritchard widows raised no objections to his plans. They agreed that they had never fully shared, or even understood, their husbands' enmity towards Jack Rimmer and they seemed content that his son was prepared to take responsibility for running the ranch – a task they had struggled with in their husbands' absence and were more than happy to relinquish.

As Abraham Mason looked down at Jack Rimmer's grave, he felt a deep sense of satisfaction at the strange chain of events which had allowed him to avenge the friend he hadn't seen for over twenty years but who, he now knew, had died illegally on the end of a rope.

Revenge was sweet, though the marshal would remain the only person to know for certain whether the pressure of his strong hands round David Pritchard's throat had truly been an act of self-defence during a legal arrest, or whether it was due to Abraham Mason's personal determination to ensure that the man in his grip suffered the same choking sensations as his buddy.

When he rode alone back to Bush Creek later, the marshal consoled himself for the loss of his one-time partner with the thought that perhaps the future wasn't going to be quite so lonely as the previous two decades. During all the recent dramatic activities and trials he had become a far less remote figure to the inhabitants of the isolated township in the Texas brush, who now accepted him as one of their own, even though they suspected he might not remain with them for ever.

And he even had a kind of surrogate family. As he had left Peterland Valley, Julie's last words had created unfamiliar emotions within him. 'Make sure you come back and see our baby,' Julie had insisted. 'Rory and me haven't got any parents, now. We want you to be a kind of grandfather to our youngster. After all, he or she will be your old buddy's grand-child.'